Gayrabian Nights

Gayrabian Nights is a twist on the well-known classic, *1001 Arabian Nights*, in which Scheherazade, under the threat of death if she ceases to captivate King Shahryar's attention, enchants him through a series of mysterious, adventurous, and romantic tales.

In this variation, a male escort, invited to the hotel room of a closeted, homophobic Mormon senator, learns that the man is poised to vote on a piece of anti-gay legislation the following morning. To prevent him from sleeping, so that the exhausted senator will miss casting his vote on the Senate floor, the escort entertains him with stories of homophobia, celibacy, mixed orientation marriages, reparative therapy, coming out, first love, gay marriage, and long-term successful gay relationships. The escort crafts the stories to give the senator a crash course in gay culture and sensibilities, hoping to bring the man closer to accepting his own sexual orientation.

Praise for Johnny Townsend

In *Gayrabian Nights*, "Townsend's prose is always limpid and evocative, and…he finds real drama and emotional depth in the most ordinary of lives."

Kirkus Reviews

Gayrabian Nights "was easily the most original book I've read all year. Funny, touching, topical, and thoroughly enjoyable."

Rainbow Awards

Gayrabian Nights is "an allegorical tour de force…a hard-core emotional punch."

Gay. Guy. Reading and Friends

In *Zombies for Jesus*, "Townsend isn't writing satire, but deeply emotional and revealing portraits of people who are, with a few exceptions, quite lovable."

Kel Munger, *Sacramento News and Review*

In *Sex among the Saints,* "Townsend writes with a deadpan wit and a supple, realistic prose that's full of psychological empathy….he takes his protagonists' moral struggles seriously and invests them with real emotional resonance."

Kirkus Reviews

Let the Faggots Burn: The UpStairs Lounge Fire is "a gripping account of all the horrors that transpired that night, as well as a respectful remembrance of the victims."

Terry Firma, Patheos

Orgy at the STD Clinic portrays "an all-too real scenario that Townsend skewers to wincingly accurate proportions…[with] instant classic moments courtesy of his punchy, sassy, sexy lead character…"

Jim Piechota, *Bay Area Reporter*

Orgy at the STD Clinic is "…a triumph of humane sensibility. A richly textured saga that brilliantly captures the fraying social fabric of contemporary life." Named to Kirkus Reviews' Best Indie Books of 2022.

Kirkus Reviews

Gayrabian Nights

Johnny Townsend

Print ISBN: 979-8-9878666-4-1
Ebook ISBN: 979-8-9878666-5-8

Second Edition
2023

Cover design by Todd Engel

Contents

The Hotel Room

It was an out call, a little late at a few minutes past 10:00. That usually meant a tourist who wanted to get laid but didn't have the energy to try the bars. The guy asked me to come to his hotel near Dupont Circle. Of course, a hotel call didn't automatically mean "tourist." Lots of rich guys just wanted a little on the side but were afraid to come to my place, though I did in calls, too. Those were easier, naturally, but to be honest, I preferred going out over bringing total strangers to my own home, if given the choice, but a struggling grad student at Georgetown couldn't afford to be too choosy.

I walked through the lobby purposefully, not going to the front desk or making eye contact with any of the staff. Many hotels tried to discourage visits such as mine, so I made an effort to get the floor and room number directly from the client. In the posh hotels that required some sort of key card to make the elevator work, the client had to wait for me in the lobby. This hotel offered easy access, though, and a few moments later, I was knocking on Room 312.

The door opened a crack. "Matt?" asked a man whose left eye was the only visible part of his body.

I smiled and said, "Yes, sir," avoiding the words, "At your service" where others might overhear and make the client nervous.

The door opened wider to reveal a man in his early forties, clean-shaven, with slightly graying, neatly combed hair, wearing a white bathrobe and slippers. He motioned for me to come in, and I did. As soon as the door closed, however, he pointed to my bag. "What's that?"

"I was a Boy Scout," I replied. "So I always come prepared. Condoms, lube, massage oil, dildo, tit clamps…"

The man thrust out his arm authoritatively. "I need to make sure there's no recorder or camera in there."

I held out the bag. Blackmail was never my game, though I knew some other escorts who tried it. Such a tiring method of obtaining funds seemed far more trouble than it was worth. I simply needed enough money to pay for two more years of school and living expenses. With my class schedule and labs scattered throughout the day, and projects keeping me working extra hours on any given night, a regular job was difficult. Besides, almost any job I could find that would actually meet my requirements would only pay a paltry wage. Selling my sexual services, I made $200 an hour.

That people were willing to pay such a price amazed me. But I was twenty-four and naturally gifted with muscular definition. Other guys at the gym would slave over exercises for weeks and months and never get the first sign of a washboard stomach. I worked out thirty minutes a day and was ripped. No steroids for me. I was lucky and I knew it, and outside of any financial need I might have that pushed me into this career, I also felt a need to "give back to the community." I felt privileged doing this work, not degraded.

"Okay, here's your bag back, Matt."

"What shall I call you?" I asked, taking the bag from him.

"Something dirty."

Oh, brother. One of those. "Cocksucker!" I said.

He smiled and I realized I recognized him. I'd seen that smile before on television, although he didn't strike me as an actor or performer. In Washington, DC, he was almost certainly a politician, and I'd had my fair share of them as clients. More Republicans than Democrats, for whatever reason.

He opened his robe. "*You're* the cocksucker," he said, revealing his half-erect penis. "Suck it!"

So we got started right away, which was fine with me. I dreaded the clients who wanted a back rub first that could take thirty or forty minutes and was excruciatingly boring. I preferred getting right down to business. Even sucking a cock, if it wasn't very responsive, could get tedious, but over the next twenty-five or thirty minutes, we tried a number of different activities, and I would have considered it a good time even if I wasn't being paid. He smelled shower-fresh, always a bonus, and wasn't overly passive and lifeless like some guys.

Usually the client was interested only in his own orgasm, but after "Cocksucker" came, he spent another five minutes making sure I ejaculated as well. That level of courtesy was rare even for the bars, much less with clients. I found myself slightly impressed.

"Lie here with your head on my chest," he commanded. I did, my ejaculate on his stomach so close that I could smell it as I rested there. He ran his fingers through my hair. "I really love your curls and your green eyes. And that hairy chest. I get really tired of the buzz cuts and shaved chests that so many guys have." I wondered just how often he did this, and then I realized I was being judgmental, hardly my place. The man put his arm around my back and sighed. "This is what I really miss," he said softly, "not the foreplay, not the sex itself, but the cuddling afterward." From my vantage point, I could just make out my jeans and shirt lying in a heap on the floor. I started planning my exit.

I didn't bother to tell him that a lot of gay guys never cuddled even in relationships. I stole a glance at a clock on the bedside table. With an exam the next morning in Radiation Medicine, I needed to get a reasonable amount of sleep if I was going to do well. Ever since my mother died of ovarian cancer when I was fourteen, I'd been determined to work in oncology, though I double majored in both English and Biology, and earned a minor in History as well. At first, I thought I'd become a physician but later decided on research. I was a year into my PhD program for Tumor Biology, and I needed to keep my grades up or risk being asked to leave the program. Usually, on nights before an exam, I wouldn't answer the cell phone I had dedicated just for this job. But it had been a slow week, with only four other calls, so I'd decided to take the assignment.

"You don't do this with your…" How could I phrase that delicately?

"With my wife?" he finished, his eyes on the ceiling. "No. I expect she would like it, too, but after we have sex, I feel so…dirty…that I just get up and go to the bathroom and wash up. When I get back in bed, I turn away from her and go to sleep."

Maybe I didn't want to know any more about this stranger. Anonymous sex could be fun, but getting to know the person behind the mouth and asshole and penis wasn't always as enjoyable.

"We have five children," he went on, "from four to sixteen. Guys sometimes kid me about all the sex my wife and I must be having." He chuckled in a cheerless sort of way. "I always use her pregnancy as an excuse to leave her alone. Frankly, I don't think she enjoys sex with me any better than I do with her. But we're Mormons, so what can we do?"

He tensed a little as he said that, as if afraid he had revealed too much. I was in fact surprised, as I'd been raised Mormon myself, though I thought I'd better not reveal that detail too quickly, for fear he'd feel awkward. Over the years, I'd had sex with Catholics, Jews, Muslims, atheists, Baptists, and even a Wiccan. There was no reason to believe there weren't lots of gay Mormons as well.

"I had a boyfriend during my undergraduate days who was Mormon," I said, feeling saddened by the memory. I still missed Derrick. He hadn't actually been Mormon, but saying so seemed a soft way of letting this guy know he wasn't alone. I had certainly learned one thing from dating so many men. Homosexuality was universal. A particular religion could create its own specific difficulties in accepting it, but reality was reality regardless.

The man turned his head toward me. "Really."

I nodded. "Where are you from?"

He hesitated for a long moment and then sighed. "Idaho."

Then it clicked. "You're Senator Sefton!"

"You won't tell, will you?" I could see his muscles tense. "I can make life very difficult for you if you do."

"Oh, there's no need to threaten," I said softly. "I provide a service, that's all. If it makes you feel any better, I stand to lose as much as you do."

"I doubt it."

"Well, I stand to lose a lot."

I listened to footsteps walking heavily down the hallway. Someone fumbled with a doorknob, and then I heard a door shut. The senator caressed my back absentmindedly, a surprisingly gentle action, I felt, for someone who'd just threatened me. After a moment, he hugged me very tightly and whispered, "Tomorrow's another big day for me."

"Why's that?" I asked.

"There's a vote in the Senate. It's on a bill about dairy subsidies."

"Sounds riveting."

"Well, someone has tacked on a bit to deny same-sex couples Social Security benefits."

"What's that got to do with the dairy industry?" I asked.

"Nothing. But that's the way politics works." He rubbed my shoulder. "I've voted against gay rights exactly eleven times in the past." He paused. "I'm a Mormon. I'm a Republican. I'm from Idaho. I *have* to vote against gay rights."

"But you don't want to?" I prodded.

"Yes," he said sadly. "I do want to. Homosexuality is bad. It's evil. Look at what it's made me do. I've cheated on my wife."

"Yes, no straight guys ever cheat on their wives."

"You know what I mean."

I straightened up so that my head was on the pillow next to Senator Sefton's pillow. "How can a bill like that even pass these days?" I asked. "Gay rights have come a long way."

"Republicans will always hate you," he replied, a tinge of bitterness in his voice. "At least, they will for the foreseeable future. And there will be bill after bill, if not on the federal level, then certainly on the state level."

I was so frustrated I almost told him what I thought of him. But he hadn't paid me yet, so I didn't want to get him too mad.

I had to do *something*, though. But what? For a second I thought of tying him up so he couldn't get away in time for the vote, except—he already knew my cell number. The police could trace it easily, even if it wasn't my main phone. A Mormon Republican from Idaho didn't sound like the type of person who would be easily influenced by logical argument, either. So what was left?

I got up on one elbow and traced his right nipple with my finger. To my surprise, he started to cry. I started to move my hand away, but Sefton pressed it against his breast. "You won't understand this," he said, sniffling. "But we Mormons wear special garments, special underwear."

"I've heard," I said, though I thought it best not to mention a certain sex game my former boyfriend and I had played when I made him wear mine.

"Did you know that over the right nipple we have an L embroidered? It stands for holding one's arm to the square, to indicate how righteous we will be as Mormons."

"Is it righteous to vote to oppress people?" I asked, trying to keep my voice calm. "To deny equal rights in a country founded upon the principle of equality?" I could hear a tinge of anger creeping into my tone. I hoped I hadn't gone too far.

"My politics are shaped more by my faith in God than my faith in the political process."

Oh, brother. While I was disgusted, I also realized this guy was in torment. I had gone through some of the same crap when I was coming out, but at least I'd gotten it over with fairly quickly, though to be fair, that might have been because I was so much younger and times had been different when I was growing up. He might not be a bad man, just tortured. And people often did bad things under torture, like give away their comrades to a tyrannical government. It happened under the Nazis. It happened under the Soviet regime. And it happened sometimes even in America.

Suddenly, I remembered a literature class I'd taken once. We'd studied Boccaccio's *Decameron*, in which a group of ten friends spent ten days in the countryside telling each other stories to while away the hours in the hope of escaping the plague. We'd also read *1001 Arabian Nights*, about the king who has become so disenchanted with women that he marries a virgin every night, has sex with her, and then executes her in the morning before she has a chance to cheat on him. Scheherazade stays alive by telling the king a captivating story every evening, but not finishing it, leaving him so intrigued he keeps her alive until the following evening. She finishes the story at that point, but then she immediately begins another one to keep him interested. She doesn't finish the new one until the following night, keeping this up for a thousand and one nights.

I'd always enjoyed literature classes, and I had always been a good storyteller around Boy Scout campfires. Could I keep Sefton awake all night by telling a succession of stories? If he didn't get enough sleep and couldn't make the vote…well, who knew if it would even make a difference? His probably wouldn't be the deciding vote in any case. There were a lot of rabidly homophobic Republican senators, and more than a handful of lukewarm Democrats. Would this experiment really be worth missing my exam in the morning?

I looked at the senator. The warm afterglow of sex seemed to be leaving his face.

I had to do something. I regularly clicked on links in emails to sign petitions sent by Credo or by the Progressive Democrats of America or by the Human Rights Campaign. Maybe those things had an effect, and maybe they didn't. But here was a chance to make a difference of at least one relevant vote. It might not be much, but it was the only thing I had any control over at this moment, if I acted fast. I had to do *something*.

Before Sefton could suggest we put our clothes on, and the mood was irrevocably broken, I strummed my fingers through his hair and said gently, "Would you like to hear a bedtime story before I leave?"

"A bedtime story? Whatever for?"

"I think you'll like it. It'll be something to remember me by."

I thought he might push my hand away and sit up, but after what appeared to be a momentary internal struggle, he relaxed, his head sinking deeper into his pillow. "Oh, all right. But make it short. I'm paying you by the hour, aren't I?"

I laughed. "You're paying for the sex," I said. "The after-dinner story is on the house."

The Boycott

Ann put down her copy of *Lysistrata* and looked at the portrait of the First Presidency hanging on the living room wall. Her eyes narrowed as she scanned the other paintings in the room. Jesus Christ and Heavenly Father talking to Joseph Smith. Peter, James, and John ordaining Joseph. Brigham Young in his wagon entering the Salt Lake valley.

Ann frowned.

She'd heard through the grapevine that the radical group Ordain Women was going to try to gain admittance to the Priesthood session of General Conference in two weeks. Ann wasn't sure even Philip would be able to attend. It was a big conference center, but there were always thousands of men trying to get in from all around the world.

Ann had talked to Philip about her feelings many, many times. Philip's response was always, "You don't *need* the priesthood. You have *me*."

It had been very difficult to raise her right hand to sustain Philip when he was called as bishop fourteen months ago. But she'd been a dutiful wife and done so. She had believed that once in a position of substance, her husband would have more influence on the larger church and be able to help enlighten people to ideas of equality.

Unfortunately, since he didn't hold those ideas himself, he was hardly the right subject to proselytize them. Still, Ann was determined to at least get Philip to say something in Sacrament meeting just once about the Church needing to reevaluate its position on women and the priesthood. And he needed to say something *before* General Conference. She was going to have to do something that left him no choice. He was already stressed to the max with both work and his clerical duties. It shouldn't take much to push him over the edge. She stared at the First Presidency and thought.

An hour later, Philip walked through the door. "Hi, honey, I'm home."

Ann walked up to meet him and kissed him gently on the lips. "How was your day, dear?"

"Tough. My boss is killing me." He took off his coat and hung it up.

"I'm so sorry."

"But I'll be boss one day soon myself."

"You're certainly cut out for it," said Ann. "I'm sorry you have to put up with him."

"Her."

"Oh, that's right."

"Well, it's nothing a plate of macaroni and cheese won't cure." Philip's eyes twinkled.

"Macaroni and cheese?" asked Ann innocently.

"It's Tuesday night, isn't it?"

"Oh, that." Ann smiled coyly. "Well, I decided that until you say in Sacrament meeting that you think women ought to be ordained to the priesthood, I'm not cooking anymore."

"What?"

"No more dinners. No more breakfasts. No more preparing your lunch to take to work."

Philip laughed nervously. "That's not even funny, Ann."

"It sure isn't."

Philip's brows furrowed. "Ann, I've had a hard day at work. I'm the breadwinner around here. I pay all the bills. It's your job to be a wife and do the cooking and housework. If I do my share, you have to do your share."

"I'd be happy to," said Ann. "Once you make the announcement."

"I'm not being excommunicated just to fulfill some stupid whim. The Church will never ordain women to the priesthood. It wasn't done in the New Testament, and it wasn't done in the Book of Mormon. It simply isn't God's will."

"If I recall," said Ann brightly, "there was no Relief Society for women in the New Testament or Book of Mormon, either. No Primary, for that matter. No Institute." She batted her eyes innocently.

Philip stormed up the stairs and slammed the bedroom door. The kids, Ben and Susan, ten and eight, had just come down the stairs as their father pushed past them. They looked at Ann questioningly.

"How about chicken nuggets for dinner?" she said with a smile.

She obviously had to feed the kids, but it would be the simplest meals possible, no matter their nutritional value. They'd remember the boycott with fondness, regardless of Philip's actions.

Philip came downstairs just as the family was finishing up. He made no attempt to open the fridge or the pantry. He simply grabbed his coat and said, "I'm going out to eat." He opened the front door. "At that restaurant on Olive you like so much." Then he was out the door.

Ann laughed.

She was in bed when she heard the car pull back up in the driveway. Philip would have had to spend most of his evening at the church meeting with the members. Members with problems. Members who would add to his stress. He came up the stairs, opened the bedroom door, and loudly clicked the light on, adjusting the dimmer so that the light shone at its brightest. He didn't say a word but noisily undressed, stomping about and slamming drawers.

Ann pretended to sleep through it all.

Philip plopped into bed roughly, trying to shake the mattress as much as possible. Ann continued to pretend to sleep. Philip kicked her in the leg, also pretending, that it was an accident.

The next morning, Ann poured cereal for the kids and sent them off to school. She was eating a bagel with cream cheese when Philip showed up in the kitchen. He poured himself some orange juice and left without saying a word. Ann was sure he'd get tired of providing his own food long before she had her fill of his spitefulness. She'd grown used to it over the years and built up a defense, since this was hardly his first display. Once, about two years ago, Ann had announced at the dinner table that she'd applied for a part-time job at the library. Philip's immediate response was to say calmly, "If you interview for that position, I'll sell the second car."

Another time, she'd mentioned that she was tired of doing genealogy at the Family History Library every Friday morning. "All the work will be done in the Millennium anyway," she'd said.

"No Family History," Philip had countered, "and no more gift cards from Barnes and Noble for you to waste all your time reading books." She'd given in that time, too. She had almost a thousand books. Philip always complained that they were taking up too much space. And it wasn't as if she couldn't borrow from the library. But owning a book felt sometimes like the only freedom she had.

Ann spent the day reading another Greek play.

Around 5:15, the front door opened. "Honey, I'm home." Philip sounded cheerful. Ann's heart skipped a beat. Had he decided to give in so soon?

"Hi, sweetie," said Ann, going up to him and giving him a kiss. "How was your day?"

"Oh, it was just fine," he said with a grin. "During lunch, I went to the bank and took your name off the account. It's not joint any more. No more money for you until you decide to act like a wife." He smiled and sauntered into the kitchen. "What's for dinner?"

"I had dinner already," said Ann sweetly. "A fried egg sandwich on toast. Boy, it really hit the spot. I know how much you like them, too."

Philip eyed her warily.

"I fed the kids early, too. They're upstairs doing their homework. Little angels." Ann had some money hidden in the house if she needed it. And Philip's new tactic simply meant that he'd have to do the shopping and cooking for the kids himself once they ran out of what was already in the house. She could live with that.

"I want dinner," said Philip flatly.

"Be my guest." Ann started out of the kitchen. "Oh, I suppose I should mention, you only have one more clean shirt. And since I'm no longer doing your laundry, so you might want to address that after you eat something." There actually had been several clean shirts still in his closet, but

Ann had deliberately wrinkled six of them and tossed them in the hamper this morning.

"Well, I'm not taking out the garbage anymore."

"I'll get over it."

"And I'm taking back the keys of the car I let you use."

"You mean, my car?" Ann played along.

"No, *my* car. Everything here is mine. I paid for everything."

"All right, dear. Since I'm not buying groceries or running errands for you all day anymore, I suppose that's fair." She started to walk away but then turned back. "I think there are some saltines in the pantry."

"There are no ordained women in the Bible or Book of Mormon!"

Ann put her finger on her chin as if contemplating. "There are no sister missionaries, either, are there? Or Visiting Teachers? Or Home Teachers? Hmm, that's odd."

Ann walked up the stairs and closed the bedroom door. This had better work, she thought, or they were headed for a divorce. Why did men have to be such buttheads? She wondered for a moment if she were doing the right thing. She didn't particularly mind being a stay-at-home mom. She honestly did think it best for one parent to be available for the children. She just didn't think it always had to be the mother. There was no reason a man couldn't stay at home and let his wife lead an exciting career. For that matter, there was no reason they couldn't both have part-time jobs and both take part in raising the kids. There was no reason she *had* to be totally, one hundred percent dependent on her husband for everything.

Ann picked up the phone and called Betty, the wife of Philip's first counselor in the bishopric. She quickly explained what she'd been doing and why, and Betty asked, "Is it working?"

"It's too soon to tell," Ann replied, "but it'll work better if you do it, too. *Someone* in the bishopric will crack."

"Are you going to call Samantha as well?" The second counselor's wife.

"As soon as I hang up with you."

"All right," said Betty, "I'll give it a try. But only till Sunday."

Ann wasn't sure she'd have success that soon, but any help was useful. She dialed Samantha next and told her what both she and Betty were up to. "Grady is such a prick sometimes," Samantha said. "Thinks his dick makes him a god. I'm with you."

"If we can keep this up for a couple of weeks," said Ann, "I'll call the stake president's wife."

"Well, she's in our ward, too. There's no reason she can't be in on this."

"She's a bit fanatical in her religious devotion," said Ann, "but I did hear her in the bathroom at church a few weeks ago say something about how she could run the stake better than Fred."

Samantha laughed. "Call me tomorrow and we'll compare notes."

Ann read until 9:30 and then turned off the light. Perhaps half an hour later, Philip came in after another evening at church, surely exhausted and stressed again. He turned the light on as bright as it would go and stomped about as he had the night before. Then he turned the light down low. Climbing into bed, he shook Ann's shoulder. "I want to make love," he declared.

This was the moment Ann had been waiting for. She'd heard about the Ukrainian women vowing not to have sex with Russian men after the takeover of Crimea. She'd read about the women in Kenya, Liberia, and Colombia having their sex strikes to force men to their will. Sometimes it worked and sometimes it didn't. She thought again of *Lysistrata*.

"Oh, honey, I'm so anxious to make love to you, too." She watched him smile and said, "And we can do that just as soon as you take a stand publicly in church that women should be ordained to the priesthood."

Philip's face grew cold. "I can divorce you, you know."

"But they won't let you be bishop any longer."

"They won't let me be bishop if I say what you want me to say."

"But you'll still have me and the kids. An eternal family."

"Honey, you have to accept the facts. God didn't ordain women in the Bible and the Book of Mormon because he didn't want them to be ordained."

"I suppose that's possible, dear," Ann said slowly, "but I can't help but recognize there was no church university in those scriptures, either. No Family Home Evening. No Word of Wisdom. No Singles wards." She paused. "Do you think it's just barely conceivable that God doesn't need us to do everything the exact way it was done two thousand years ago?"

Philip deflated in front of her eyes, and Ann almost felt sorry for him. "I'm so tired," he mumbled.

"I'm thirty-two years old," Ann returned, "and I've heard every day of my life that I'm not equal to men. You've had two hard days and *you* think *you're* tired!"

Philip sighed heavily. "All right. All right. I'll say something in Sacrament meeting this Sunday. Satisfied?"

"I will be on Sunday."

"So can we forget about all this and get our lives back to normal?'

"Not until after Sacrament meeting on Sunday," said Ann. And maybe not even then, she realized. She wasn't sure that a one-time announcement was going to make any kind of significant change in the Church. Maybe she should keep this up, and spread it by word of mouth from one bishopric to another to another. People had cousins and sisters and friends in other wards and stakes across the country. Maybe she could get a real movement going. Perhaps no one should give in until there was real change, even if it took a year.

People said it would be at least fifty more years before the Church started treating women equally. But if even twenty percent of the women stopped having sex with their men, it would sure happen a lot sooner.

"All right. It's just a few more days. I'll go beat off in the bathroom." Philip started to climb out of bed.

"While you're in there," said Ann to his back as he walked away, "be thinking about your brothers and college roommates and former mission companions you can call tomorrow. You can ask them to say something in Sacrament meeting, too. They can offer to give talks or something. Your calling them is part of the deal, too."

She watched Philip hunch over at the words, but he didn't turn around. "Okay, honey."

She could hardly hear him.

Then he went in the bathroom and closed the door. Was this what power felt like, Ann mused. No wonder men didn't want to share it.

But sharing good things always made those things better. Ann would share. She pulled the blanket up closer to her chin, thought of new ways to torment her husband, and smiled.

The Hotel Room

"What the hell was that!?" asked Sefton, looking at me with a horrified expression.

"I thought Mormons didn't curse," I said with a smile.

"And I thought you weren't Mormon."

"Well, my Mormon boyfriend and I did talk quite at length about his religion."

"So it would seem." He shook his head and exhaled heavily. "And just what was the point of that story?"

To be honest, I'd hoped to show him that even heterosexual relationships didn't always work out very well, and maybe gay sex wasn't the worst thing in the world. It was clear Sefton both loved and hated sex at the same time. I'd also hoped a little humor would make the ideas go down more easily. Judging by his consternation, I wasn't so sure I'd succeeded.

I didn't know how many stories I would have a chance to tell, but I'd chosen to start with something not technically gay, which might make him believe I wasn't trying to manipulate him to identify with my characters and what they were doing. Yet he'd feel what I wanted him to feel regardless, and that was the important thing.

"Do you think you can tell a better story?" I asked. My strategy to detain Sefton would be more effective if I could entice him to actively participate. My life might not be at stake the way Scheherazade's was, but my quality of life certainly was. Perhaps even my actual life might be to a degree, since homophobia in politics and religion led directly to homophobia in society, and I would never forget that Derrick had been stabbed to death by a gay basher two years ago, the day after he'd been accepted to medical school.

It mattered what happened on the Senate floor tomorrow.

"No," he said, "I suppose not. I've never been very good at telling stories." He paused. "Except for the ones I tell my wife. It's easy enough when I'm in Washington. And I never fool around when I'm back home. But she phones sometimes when I should be in my apartment here in the city. When I don't answer, she gets upset, which calls for some fancy wordplay later."

"What do you tell her?"

"Sometimes, I say I'm having a late dinner with another senator. Or maybe I'll say I just had to go out for a breath of fresh air and forgot to check the answering machine when I got back in."

"Doesn't she call your cell?"

"Cell phones can be intercepted too easily. I prefer land lines."

"You don't think she ever gets suspicious?"

"I don't know. I suppose she does, though I expect she thinks it's another woman. We don't talk about it. It's always kind of hovering in the air, but we simply pretend there's nothing there."

That sounded like a perfectly dreadful way to live. But it was his life, and I wasn't a marriage counselor.

"The real difficulty," he went on, "is the time difference between DC and Idaho. When it's bedtime here, it's still early enough for Becky to call to hear my voice before *she* goes to bed. So it's tricky getting out. I just tell her that I turn off the ringer once I'm in bed."

"Does it ever occur to you that Becky might be having an affair herself?" I asked.

Sefton laughed, a condescending sound. "I wish she would. There would be a scandal, of course, if we divorced, but if I were no longer married, I wouldn't feel I was sinning so much. I could be a bachelor—at least for a few years—without anyone questioning." He sighed. "It would be heaven."

With a glance at his wrist, Sefton realized his watch was somewhere else in the room. He hadn't been paying much attention when I took it off earlier along with his other clothing, staring so intently at me at the time. He squinted his eyes now to look at the clock on the bedside table. Not a good sign. I decided to take some action. "I think I can tell this next story better," I said.

"There's going to be a next story? It's getting late."

"It's okay. This is a short one. You'll like it." I kissed his ear, and he smiled as if I'd embarrassed him.

"All right," he said. "Let's hear your story."

Bumper Sticker Theology

"Are you sure you won't come?" Henry asked. "You can go as you are. It's casual." At forty-three, Elizabeth could still look stunning when she wanted to. And he certainly didn't want to go today looking like a single forty-five-year-old man. He stood at the door with one hand on the knob, afraid to open it.

"No," Elizabeth said coldly. "And I'm still debating whether or not to call the bishop."

"Oh, Elizabeth, you know I have no choice."

"There's always a choice between sinning and not sinning."

"I have no choice!" Henry opened the door, quickly walked through it, and shut it behind him firmly. Mormon wives were supposed to support their husbands, he thought angrily. He was the breadwinner in the family, after all. Elizabeth shouldn't be so hard-nosed.

He sat behind the wheel in his PT Cruiser. The car had been so hip when it first came out, but then the market had become glutted, and the manufacturer never did come out with any daring new models. Just the one. Henry, though, had bought the vehicle before everyone jumped on the bandwagon. *He* was adventurous.

Henry grumbled as he pulled away from the house. Driving from Fremont in north Seattle up to Mukilteo was going to be such a pain. Derek and Jordan lived reasonably nearby in Seward Park. There was no reason the ceremony had to be held way up on Whidbey Island. It was just like gay people to make life difficult for everyone around them.

Derek was Henry's boss at Costco, heading one of the HR divisions. He was nice enough, but he had his own way of looking at things, and heaven forbid anyone thought differently. To be honest, Henry usually agreed with him on most things, but he could never shake the feeling that he was just a yes man, going along with everything because he was afraid of losing his job. Derek hadn't actually ordered Henry to attend his wedding, but three other people from the department were going, and Henry felt it was better to be safe than sorry.

Traffic was thick and slow, lots of people trying to get away from the city for the weekend. It was the first week of July, around 68 degrees, without a cloud in the sky. Perfect weather for an outing.

Damn Elizabeth for making this even harder than it had to be.

An SUV passed by in the lane to his right. Henry noticed the bumper sticker on the rear of the vehicle. "One man, one woman. As God intended. Vote no on Ref. 74." Henry groaned. He had a similar bumper sticker on the back of his own car. He'd tried to peel it off a couple of days ago in order to be ready for today, but the infernal thing was stuck permanently. If only the citizens of Seattle weren't overly ripe for destruction, they would have voted against the referendum. In his rear view mirror, Henry could see Mt. Rainier towering above everything, its top half so high that even in the middle of summer it was still covered in snow. And ahead and to the right, he could see Mt. Baker, also covered in snow. Heavenly Father would surely make one of the volcanoes erupt before long, or cause another big earthquake, or a tsunami, or *something*. This much wickedness couldn't go on unchecked forever.

After almost an hour, Henry arrived in Mukilteo. He didn't get in the line for the ferry but drove straight to the parking area. He was going on as a foot passenger. Derek had offered the option of being chauffeured in a van from the ferry station on the other side, and Henry had jumped at the chance. It took fifteen minutes to find a parking space, and just as Henry bought his $4.65 ticket, he heard the gate closing. He'd just missed the ferry. Thirty minutes now until the next one.

Perhaps that was Heavenly Father giving him another chance to back out. There were supposed to be fifty people at the wedding. Derek wouldn't miss him. Henry could come up with some excuse.

Liars went to the Telestial Kingdom, the lowest degree of heaven.

Henry was going to the Celestial Kingdom, the highest degree. Only those with a temple marriage could go there. There was talk that good people who'd never found a lifemate could also reach the Celestial Kingdom, but Henry wasn't sure those folks wouldn't instead be relegated to ministering angel status rather than godhood like he and Elizabeth would be.

All this talk of legalizing same sex marriage was ridiculous. Nothing outside of the temple mattered anyway. Not even regular heterosexual marriages performed in city halls or churches or synagogues counted. Heavenly Father was quite explicit on the subject.

Derek was Jewish. What chance did he have in any event? And Jordan was an atheist. It was laughable that Henry was afraid of losing his job when these men had lost both salvation and exaltation.

Three gay men had appeared near the gate, waiting for the next ferry as well. They looked enough like real men, Henry supposed, but he could just *tell*. Something about the way they joked and laughed. They seemed too happy, the way only people who had no thought for the consequences of their actions could.

Just before 3:00, Henry looked up and saw the ferry approaching. The water churned heavily as it came to a stop. Workers tied ropes and let down a ramp. Then about twenty people walked off, followed by a horde of vehicles. Henry walked on next, trailing behind the gay men. There was also an obese woman laughing with them now. Henry had heard that lesbians were fat. This woman looked straight, though, probably just friendless because of her weight and willing to accept anyone who talked to her.

Henry climbed two flights of stairs and headed to the front of the ferry, where there was a tiny landing surrounded by a guard rail. As the ferry started out across the water, Henry luxuriated in the feel of the strong breeze against his face. His shirt was billowing in the wind, and the temperature out here felt at least ten degrees cooler than it had on land. He looked at the tiny whitecaps on the water, and the island rising majestically out of the Sound ahead of him. Such beauty. The Celestial Kingdom must be something like this.

Derek and Jordan had better enjoy it while they could.

Henry watched as the houses along the shore of Whidbey Island grew larger. He always enjoyed ferry rides. He'd gone to Vashon and Bainbridge and even up to Victoria in British Columbia with Elizabeth and the two boys. It was always fun.

He grinned now, remembering a song he and his friends used to sing on the school bus on the way to middle school. The bus driver was named Mrs. Jolly, and her son rode the bus, too. Henry and the others used to sing every day, "Hooray for the bus driver, the bus driver, the bus driver. Hooray for the bus driver, the bus driver, hooray. She's Jolly, she's merry, her kid is a fairy. Hooray for the bus driver, the bus driver, the bus driver. Hooray for the bus driver, the bus driver, hooray."

Henry wondered whatever became of that kid.

Probably died of AIDS years ago.

Henry used to wonder why the bus driver had allowed them to keep singing that song. He finally realized it was probably because she felt it would knock the boy back in line. She allowed those lyrics every day because she loved her son. You always had to make it clear to gay people that you didn't accept their choices in life. It was the only way to help them.

Was Henry selling his soul by attending this wedding?

Once on the island, Henry followed the small group, hoping they knew where the van was waiting. The three men and one woman had been joined now by another woman, young and pretty, clearly straight. Henry didn't recognize her from work, but perhaps she was a friend of Jordan's. Jordan worked in technical writing at Costco, so Henry rarely saw him there. The group walked toward a red van, and when Henry drew close enough, he could see a sign reading "Derek" against the windshield. He hurried and joined the others as they were climbing into the van.

"Hi," said one of the gay men as Henry sat next to him. The man offered his hand. Henry shook it unhappily. "I'm Joey."

"Henry," said Henry.

Everyone else introduced themselves. Henry felt more and more tainted as the van drove on. He tried to focus on the scenery, the winding roads, the fir trees with their branches turning the roads into tunnels. After a few miles, the driver veered onto a gray gravel road, and the branches formed an even darker canopy. Soon they were so deep into the wildnerness that the road had grass growing between the wheel ruts. Henry worried for a moment if this was all a trick of some kind, a kidnapping to get innocent people deep into the woods to rape them.

Eventually, they pulled up to a bland looking house, really just a double-wide mobile home with siding added. There was also a huge garage almost as big as the house. Lots of people were milling about. Henry wished Elizabeth were here.

She was home helping Steven practice his going away talk. Their 18-year-old had been called to serve a mission in Quebec and would be leaving in a few weeks. He'd be giving his talk not tomorrow, which was Fast and Testimony day, but the following Sunday. Elizabeth wanted to make sure he did a good job. She was being the real parent this weekend, while Henry was just being a good employee.

What had President David O. McKay said? No other success can compensate for failure in the home.

Well, the boy was going on a mission, wasn't he? Henry hadn't done too bad a job. And Dane was still attending Seminary classes and preparing for his turn in two more years.

Dane was a worry, though. Even though he was sixteen now and old enough to date, he'd never asked a single girl out. He seemed masculine enough, however. He played basketball at church, soccer at the school, and liked math. Surely, there was nothing wrong with him. He always laughed when Henry recounted his story of singing on the school bus as a child. Or when he told Steven and Dane about the time he and some other boys pulled the pants down on a boy in their ninth-grade gym class. They were in the locker room, and the boy always looked at Henry when he was changing clothes, so he'd finally gotten his friends to help. They'd pulled Randy's pants down around his ankles, and then every one of the seven other boys had hit Randy in the balls, leaving him writhing on the ground when they were finished.

The boy never came back to school again.

Henry frowned. Well, it wasn't all that different from what Mitt Romney had done, was it?

You had to be firm with gays. They thought they deserved the world. You had to teach them their place. Otherwise, it was like letting Lance Armstrong get away with doping. No one would stop speeding if the police never issued any tickets. Unless you made it clear something was unacceptable, people were just going to keep doing it.

Was it too late to take the van back to the ferry terminal? It was too far to walk, and Henry couldn't remember the way in any event.

He was stuck.

"Please, Heavenly Father, please make this wedding go poorly," Henry prayed silently. "Please teach them a lesson."

There were several cars parked in the driveway. As Henry passed them on his way to the back yard, he read a bumper sticker on a blue hybrid. "Love ALL families." Henry groaned. He walked past the first table beside the garage, filled with Costco vodka and Costco wine. There were also two dozen beer bottles. A huge glass container looked to be filled with sliced lemons in ice water. And there were six large bottles of Perrier water.

On a table next to the beverages were a few platters with food: toasted slices of a tiny bread, each slice the size of an old-fashioned silver dollar; chunks of various cheeses with cheese knives next to them; olives and cherries; and tiny skewers with two grape tomatoes surrounding a tiny mozzarella ball on each one.

But the best thing of all was the flies. They were *everywhere*. Flies on the food. Flies on the drinks. Flies on the faces of all the people. Everyone was waving away flies non-stop.

God had sent a plague. How wonderful! God understood. God was going to do the right thing even if Henry was weak. Henry knew he had a good story for tomorrow's Fast and Testimony meeting at church. He felt the Holy Spirit testifying to him.

Henry made his way to Derek, who was petting a mongrel dog. "Congratulations on your special day," said Henry, shaking Derek's hand.

"Thank you for coming," said Derek, swiping away at a fly.

Henry stood off to the side and just observed everyone else for a few moments. Derek introduced some people to his mother, an ancient woman who looked very frail. Derek couldn't be any older than Henry, so it was surprising to see such an old woman. Derek must have been her baby. Spoiled, no doubt. That certainly helped explain the homosexuality. And Jordan was introducing people to his mother, an attractive woman probably around sixty but looking younger. Jordan was probably around thirty-five. He had a slightly British accent, but Henry always figured the man was just affected.

Jordan saw him looking in his direction and waved him over. Henry figured he might as well play his part if he was going to be there. He shook Jordan's mother's hand, noting with surprise that she had an accent, too. "Where are you from?" he asked.

"Capetown," the woman replied. "I'm so happy I could make it for Jordan and Derek's wedding. And Enid came up from Los Angeles in the middle of her chemotherapy. She didn't want to miss this." She nodded in the direction of Derek's mother.

Henry was dumbfounded. These guys had invited their parents? And they'd actually come? Well, there were clearly no fathers about. Henry supposed they might be dead, but it seemed just as likely that these overindulgent mothers had come alone.

There were three large plastic tables set up with about six or seven chairs around each one. They were covered by large tents. Elsewhere on the lawn, people lounged on several red and white plaid blankets. Henry took a walk around the property by himself to avoid having to talk too much. He noticed, of course, the thick woods all about, huge trees maybe two or three feet apart, the property almost too thickly wooded to walk. Only the immediate yard was cleared of trees, and even here, there were three fig trees and a crabapple tree. Tiki torches burned at intervals, but they clearly weren't scaring away any of the insects. In front of the house was a green hammock, the rear wheels and rusted axle of a wagon, a pair of antlers propped on a box, and several trees covered in silk caterpillar webs, repulsive.

A heterosexual couple was walking along with their three-year-old daughter. Teaching the child at this impressionable age that gay weddings were normal. Henry made his way back to the rear of the house and hoped the ceremony would begin soon. He looked at his watch and gritted his teeth.

A server came around with a tray and offered Henry a doughy object. "It's phyllo dough with brie and sliced pears. Careful. They're hot." Henry took one and bit carefully into it, waving at his mouth with his hand. He was supposed to be fasting, but he had to try to fit in.

"Good, aren't they?" said a woman near him. She had a tattoo. Henry wondered if she was a lesbian.

Henry nodded and moved to a table where there was an empty seat. It looked like all the tables with normal heterosexuals were already filled. These people all pretended to be so tolerant, Henry sneered, but the gays were still all sitting by themselves. Such liberal hypocrites. Henry didn't feel like sitting on the grass, so he took a deep breath and went to the gay table. He waved a fly from his face.

The men next to him at the table were talking and laughing. Henry tried to ignore them, but part of their conversation caught his ear. "I was in southern Italy for New Year's," said one man with a slightly bushy beard. "I think that's where the saying, 'Out with the old, in with the new,' comes from. Everyone throws out their old furniture and stuff from their windows. People have to park their cars off the street to protect them."

"When I lived in San Francisco," said another man, clean-shaven but heavily muscled, "the people there threw out old calendars on New Year's Eve. Of course, in the Castro, they threw out Colt calendars. I used to pick them up and save them."

Everyone laughed. Henry wasn't sure what they were talking about. Probably something about bestiality and gay men.

He sure wished Elizabeth had come, if for no other reason than they'd have something to talk about later. They had so little to talk about these days. Steve and Dane. And what the bishop had said during Sacrament meeting.

Well, that was plenty.

Henry tried to ignore the flies and the talk, and about forty-five minutes later, a fat woman sat on a chair in a little clearing and started playing a harp. Then a well-dressed woman around thirty stood in front of a fig tree covered in Chinese lanterns, holding a book. Two women, one a knockout with deep auburn hair and a hunter green dress, walked up and stood to one side of the lady holding the book, and two men in dark suits walked up and stood to her other side. Then Derek walked out slowly, holding his mother's arm, followed by Jordan, holding his mother's arm.

The two mothers sat down at a table, and all the others in the wedding party stood in front of the fig tree. The lady with the book started speaking, "We gather here today to witness the union of two people who love each other."

Henry managed not to groan loudly enough to be overheard. The woman made a few more remarks and then said, "And now I'd like to read Pablo Neruda's Sonnet 17." She did read it, and it was lovely enough, but it didn't compare to looking at an infinity of mirrors pointing toward each other in the temple as one knelt at a padded altar in front of a man who held the keys to eternity. It was sad, really, to watch these ignorant people who thought they had something special when they truly only had such an inferior brand of love. The worst part was that they didn't even realize it. It was like watching a poor beggar eat a slice of stale Safeway bread, having no concept that he could have a slice of rich Rosemary Diamante bread from QFC instead. It was like someone eating a Little Debbie raisin pie when he could have a slice of The Cheesecake Factory's pumpkin cheesecake instead. It was like eating a can of Spaghetti-O's instead of lasagna from his favorite restaurant Il Fornaio.

It wasn't like these people were eating *dirt*, of course. What they were eating was edible enough. It just wasn't the delicacy that he and Elizabeth were used to. And Henry knew both Derek and Jordan well enough to be quite aware their love was far from perfect. They complained about each other all the time. Henry had been coerced to go to a couple of parties at their home in Seward Park. Derek was always bemoaning Jordan's moodiness, and Henry had heard Jordan a time or two talk about Derek's insensitivity.

But here they were, trying to make a political statement that their love was equal to anyone else's.

They were only kidding themselves.

The woman with the book was still talking. "Derek and Jordan met over fourteen years ago in London at a 'gentlemen's club.'"

Everyone laughed. Did that mean "bar"? What was so funny?

"And they've worked hard to build a relationship ever since. Jordan has had to go back to South Africa twice because of visa issues, but now with the Supreme Court ruling on DOMA, the United States will officially recognize Derek and Jordan's marriage, and Jordan can finally get a green card."

Special rights. That's all gays seemed to be after. Henry tried to keep a blank face as the ceremony continued. He waved away a fly. Soon the woman with the book was having each of the grooms repeat their vows, and then the two men kissed.

Henry had been prepared for it, so he didn't flinch.

And that was it. They were done. Henry breathed a sigh of relief and wondered when the van would start carrying people back to the ferry terminal. A long-haired man, a frumpy woman, and another man with wild white hair started playing music, a slow song, and Derek and Jordan danced while everyone cheered. Henry wondered if he could sneak another of those phyllo dough things from the catering table. Near the end of the song, Derek asked the crowd to join in the dance, and about ten couples complied, almost three quarters of them heterosexual couples. Why were so many heterosexuals celebrating a gay wedding? It just didn't make sense.

There was no van. The little girl chased the mongrel dog. Derek and Jordan danced some more. And the band kept playing, a few French songs now. Then one of the men who'd been in a suit during the wedding took the microphone away from the long-haired man and sang the old 1970's classic, "If," by Bread. He did a pretty decent job of it, even if his mannerisms were a little effeminate. Then he returned the mike back to the bandleader, but before the long-haired man could start singing again, Derek waved at the audience.

"You might have noticed all the picnic baskets as you came in," he began. "Each one has someone's name on it, and they each have plates, cups, and utensils inside. They're our gift to you for sharing with us your gift of love. Go pick up your baskets, and the caterers are bringing out dinner right now."

Henry had wondered about the baskets when he first arrived. He waited for the crowd to die down and then walked over. Sure enough, there was a wicker picnic basket with his name on a card. The gesture touched him, but then he remembered that Costco had put these baskets on sale about a month ago. He picked up his basket, waited in line at the food table, and grabbed an eggplant sandwich on French bread, a salad, and a slice of pineapple sprinkled with a touch of cinnamon. He sat back at his table, swatted at a couple of flies, and began eating.

Henry looked at his food, and the others at the table seemed to understand that he didn't want to talk and didn't try to engage him. The only problem was that he could still hear them. One woman talked about how she had marched in the Gay Pride parade the year before as part of the Catholics for Marriage Equality contingent. But then, Henry had always known that the Catholic Church was the whore of Babylon. Then, after about twenty or thirty minutes of irritating political comments, four of the men at the table started talking about how they met.

"Jeff and I met in the bushes at Volunteer Park," said the man with the slightly bushy beard.

"Do you remember the date?" asked one of the other men, slim, with a tattoo of barbed wire on his upper arm.

The first man laughed. "Of course. That's our anniversary."

"Our first date was a little more conventional," said the other man with the barbed wire tattoo. "We met in the back room of the Eagle. That's the date we celebrate, too."

This was true love? Henry had taken just about as much as he could bear of all this. The flies were in *his* face, too, because he was sinning as much as anyone else by being here. What should he do, he wondered. What would Joseph Smith do in his place?

"We've been together twelve years."

"Seventeen for us."

Henry felt his face flush. This was intolerable. Joseph Smith would testify, that's what he'd do. So would Parley P. Pratt. They never bothered to fear for their safety. The truth was what was important to them because that was what was important to God.

Abinadi spoke the truth without worrying about the consequences. So did Nephi.

If Elizabeth did report him to the bishop, Henry could say he'd borne his testimony to the crowd, that he talked of true marriage, that he'd stood up for what was right when he might be the solitary righteous person in attendance.

But he might also by his courage bring down the Holy Ghost upon the crowd, like Ammon did for King Lamoni. Dozens of people might be brought to repentance and end up being baptized.

Henry just needed to be strong and brave.

Henry stood and moved purposefully away from the table. He walked past the food trays and headed toward the band. They were taking a break, and the microphone was standing unattended. He could do this. He could really do this.

Elizabeth would stop being so negative all the time.

It would put Steven in the right spirit for his mission.

It would cure whatever might be Dane's problem.

And Henry would have a *great* story to tell in Fast and Testimony meeting.

This might even be the one act he needed to perform to have his calling and election made sure. It would take a lot of guts, but Henry already had a temple recommend. It meant he was already doing all of the "normal" good things he was supposed to be doing. Lots of them.

But this would be a *great* thing.

So what if he lost his job? So what if people laughed? He wasn't going to be like those weaklings in Lehi's dream who let go of the iron rod because people in the great and spacious building were jeering at them.

Henry felt downright filthy being at this God-forsaken gay wedding. He needed to cleanse himself. He was going to turn this obstacle into a stepping stone.

He picked the microphone out of its stand and held it to his lips.

His legs were trembling.

He was a great man.

Henry could see several people looking at him curiously. Even Derek and Jordan were looking his way. His heart was pounding. He cleared his throat.

"I just want to wish the happy couple another wonderful fourteen years," said Henry. "And another fourteen after that."

People clapped politely, and Henry hurried to the beverage table and grabbed a cup of lemon water. As he was gulping it down hurriedly, spilling half on his shirt, he saw the red van pull up out front. He dropped his cup on the ground and almost ran to be first getting in.

The guys who'd had sex with horses in San Francisco slid into the van after him, one of them pressing his leg against Henry's. A straight couple also pushed their way in. Henry ignored the chatter between the others and stared out the window till they were at the terminal. Then he lagged behind so he could wait for the ferry apart from the small group.

When the ferry finally came, about fifteen people walked off, followed by some motorcycles and a bevy of cars. One had a bumper sticker that read, "Coexist," made up of various religious symbols. It barely registered in the back of Henry's mind. He walked aboard with determination and stood at the railing on top, clutching it tightly. Soon the breeze picked up, and he watched the whitecaps as Mukilteo slowly approached across the

Sound. Henry looked at Mt. Baker in the distance, and at Mt. Rainier.

Gay people were so wicked, he thought bitterly. So self-indulgent and weak. They brought everyone down around them.

Henry waved at something in front of his eyes, though he couldn't see just what it was.

He thought about what he might say in Fast and Testimony meeting tomorrow. He was going to give a good talk. Elizabeth and the boys would be proud.

Henry brushed in irritation again at his face, though there were no flies anywhere about.

The Hotel Room

"I thought you said that story was going to be shorter," said Sefton after I concluded.

I gave him an impish grin. "I just wanted to be around you longer," I said, hoping he believed me. He smiled in return. While that was encouraging, I'd seen people living in such denial snap over the smallest things. I still felt I had to walk delicately through the minefield, trying not to detonate anything right at my feet while still identifying the mines so they could be destroyed later.

"You and your boyfriend must have talked a *lot* about Mormonism."

I smiled but said nothing.

"I don't approve of gay marriage, you know."

"Yes, I know."

There was silence for a long moment. He looked at his wedding ring.

"How long have you been doing this, Matt?" asked Sefton. "Escorting?"

"A couple of years."

"Do you like it?"

"I meet a lot of interesting guys I'd never have met any other way." I pointed at him playfully. I felt like an idiot flirting with him, but if that's what it took to keep him here all night, I was willing to do it. Odd how that felt dirtier than having sex for money did.

"You ever think about being an aide up on Capitol Hill? I could pull a few strings."

"Oh, God, no!" I said, laughing.

Sefton's face grew serious. "Please don't take the Lord's name in vain."

"Sorry."

"Have you ever been arrested?" he asked quietly.

"For escorting?" I returned. "No."

"For anything else?"

I hesitated. It wasn't good to give out too much personal information on these assignments. "Once I got caught smoking a joint."

"Oh!"

"You disapprove of marijuana?"

"I disapprove of almost everything."

"And you enjoy living like that?" I asked.

"I don't know that we're supposed to enjoy life," he replied. "We're supposed to do the right thing."

I looked at him quizzically. "I've had plenty of fun doing the right thing. Haven't you ever helped build a house with Habitat for Humanity? That's always fun. Or cleared invasive species from a state park? That's fun, too."

"Doesn't sound like it. But I've never done any of those things, anyway."

"Why not?"

"In politics, your whole life is scheduled. There's no time."

"And before you were in politics?" I asked.

"I was always teaching Sunday school or acting as First Counselor in the Bishopric of my ward or going to some meeting or other."

"Weren't any of those things fun?"

Sefton sighed. "I suppose. I kind of liked teaching Sunday school. I had the fifteen- and sixteen-year-olds. I could never really relax and enjoy the kids, though. I was always too afraid one of them would figure me out. Kids have an instinct about these things."

I remembered the kids teasing me in high school.

"And I could never stop worrying about what their parents would say if they knew."

I nodded.

"Hiding is so tiresome. But if the alternative is to be discovered, I pick hiding."

I decided we needed to lighten the atmosphere a bit. Sefton certainly needed it, and I did, too. His attitude was starting to depress me. Even if I could convince him to stay all night with me, I wasn't sure I could handle his company for that long. I was trying to be an influence on him, but he might end up being a stronger influence on me. I'd had to start taking anti-depressants after Derrick was murdered, and I'd been pill-free for almost six months now. I'd read a book, *Proof of Heaven*, about a neurosurgeon's near-death experience, and the man had been told that the universe was filled with vast amounts of love and only trace amounts of evil. It only *seemed* as if evil was everywhere, but love was really the predominant force.

Homophobia was one of those things that made me feel evil was more powerful than good. Sexism made me feel that, too. And racism. And classism. And those things seemed to be just about everywhere. I wondered if I was living in denial myself sometimes when I pretended that I could live a good, happy life as an out man.

Sefton was making my doubts return. I was afraid I might be sacrificing my own mental stability for a chance to eliminate one solitary homophobic vote.

"How about another story?" I suggested.

Sefton shrugged apathetically, and I took a deep breath and started.

The Removal of Debra

"Gary, could you type up this bid for the job I'm hoping to get? Your mom's not feeling well."

"Sure, Dad."

I followed him to his office, the former dining room which now had a desk, two file cabinets, an adding machine, and a wall lined with trophies from tractor pulls. Dad was Texas State Champion in his category. I'd only gone to one of the tractor pulls he competed in, though Mom went to almost all of them. Her favorite song was Petula Clark's "Downtown," so I wasn't sure what she thought of the rural crowds. The one pull I'd gone to was in Mississippi, just two hours north of our home in New Orleans, but it so bored me I could never force myself to go again. I felt bad not to be more supportive of him, so I was glad to be of some help now.

"Here's the proposal, Gary," Dad said, handing me several papers. "You're the college student. Fix any problems you find with it."

"Well, I don't know anything about building houses. If there's something wrong, I won't know it. I'll just type it like I see it."

"Okay. Your mom never has any trouble with it, so I guess it'll be okay."

I took the proposal upstairs to my computer and started typing. It was mostly a long list of materials or jobs and the corresponding price for each. "Molding" was one of the items. I wasn't sure if it should be "moulding," so despite what I'd told my dad about not making corrections, I thought I'd look it up. Then there was an entry for "wainscoating," and I wasn't even sure what that was, so I definitely had to look the term up. And finally I saw an entry for "the removal of debra," and that one stumped me.

My mom's name was Debra. Obviously, there wasn't a fee for getting her off the property. But was there some other person who was stalking the workers and who had to be removed from the site by a security guard? My dad had had two houses he was building burned by an arsonist once. Or was this just some technical term I wasn't aware of? My dad only had a high school education, but he was certainly intelligent enough to use some technology. He'd had faxes and cell phones and email for years.

I was just about to go downstairs and ask him about the entry when a light went off in my head, and I laughed at myself for being so slow. It was obviously supposed to be "the removal of debris."

I finished typing up the bid and handed it to my father. We got along well enough, but we never seemed to have much in common. He liked football and hunting. I liked books and movies. He liked raising cows on our land in Mississippi. I liked playing Scrabble with friends. So it felt good to have at least this one brief moment when we were working together on the same thing.

If he ever realized I was gay, of course, God only knew how he'd react to me then. I had hoped my missionary work would change me, but now I realized being gay was permanent, and I was simply doomed to Outer Darkness. Yet I still hoped as a Sunday school teacher and stake missionary to help save some other souls, even if my own was damned. I wanted my parents to make it to the Celestial Kingdom, so I didn't want to be a stumbling block to them in any way, and I tried hard to be good. If I could do some little thing for Dad today to help him, even if it was just for his business, then I felt happy about that.

"Thanks, Gary," said my dad as I handed him the papers. "I'll take a quick look at this, and then we're going to have to take your mom to the doctor."

"Is she feeling worse? I'll go in and check on her."

"No, she wants to be alone."

"Oh, okay. But you're sure you don't want me to take her? I have a test tomorrow, but I can study in the waiting room while she's with the doctor."

"No, I'll take care of it."

I was only a sophomore at the University of New Orleans, though I was 21. I was behind everyone else because I'd served two years as a Mormon missionary in Romania. I still lived at home, and Dad paid my tuition. I had a part-time job delivering pizza on Friday and Saturday nights, but I felt pretty useless most of the time, like a leech living off my parents. I did the family's laundry every few days, but it was really the only chore I did around the house.

I went back to my room and studied a little of my notes on *Hamlet*. I was going over one of the soliloquies when I heard the car pulling out of the driveway. Mom had been kind of sullen the past few weeks and clearly didn't feel well. She was the type who got grumpy when she felt ill, so I'd mostly been staying out of her way. She had a cliché personality when she had her monthly periods. She'd be fine one day and a monster the next. I'd never told her, "I guess it's that time of month" because I knew if I said it during "that time," she'd probably knock my head off. The rest of the month, she was as sweet as could be. The last few weeks, though, she'd been pretty grumpy all the time. Once, she'd even kicked our Chihuahua for getting in her way, and she loved that dog.

I had finished reviewing *Hamlet* and had moved on to *Coriolanus* when I heard the car pulling back into the driveway. I went downstairs. The kitchen door opened and Dad came in. "Where's Mom?"

Dad looked very tired. "They admitted her to the hospital. She's lost a lot of blood."

"She's hurt? I thought she was sick."

Dad gave me a weary look. "She's been bleeding for a month. I came back to get you and see if you wanted to go to the hospital to keep her company while I do some work in the office. She still doesn't want company, but I think it's best."

"Sure, Dad. Which hospital is she in?"

"Lakeside Women's Hospital."

"Okay, I'll go right now."

"You better eat a sandwich first. I won't be able to get back for a few hours."

I quickly shoved down a turkey sandwich and drove over to the hospital near my old high school. Soon I was in my mom's room. She was glaring at the bag of blood attached by a tube to her arm.

"How're you feeling?"

"Like crap," she said angrily. "I'm watching that blood go into my arm drop by drop, and I lose it as fast as it comes in. They're going to do a hysterectomy tomorrow morning."

Wow. This was serious. "What's wrong?" I asked.

"I've had fibroid tumors for years, and apparently now they're causing this bleeding."

"Well, at least you won't have periods any more. That'll be good."

My mom shot me a dirty look. "I've had periods since I was 10. I'm 43 now. I'm happy to get rid of all that junk. I'll be so glad not to have these fucking problems anymore."

I was shocked at her language. I'd once heard her say "shit" and another time heard Dad say "damn" and was surprised even at that. Mom must really be feeling awful to be in such a foul mood.

We didn't talk much for the next few hours. Finally, around 9:30, I thought I might better head back home so I could get some sleep before my morning classes started. But Mom looked so miserable I didn't want to leave her. I wondered where my dad was. I'd thought he was going to come back to see her for a little while.

At 9:45, Dad walked into the room. "You can go on now, Gary. I'll stay the night."

I nodded and gave my mom a kiss on the forehead. She looked too exhausted to be annoyed. I was surprised my dad was staying the whole night. He was not an overly demonstrative man, and this seemed much more intimate an action from him than I would have expected. I hoped my mom wasn't in any real danger.

It was hard to concentrate on my exam the next day, knowing my mom was in surgery, but I thought I did well. Mom always liked to hear about my grades, and I didn't want to let her down. After classes were over, I headed back to the hospital.

Dad was still there, though it was after 3:00 now. "How're you feeling?" I asked Mom.

"Like crap."

"I'm going to the job to get some work done. You'll want to fix a sandwich for yourself when you get home, Gary."

"Sure, Dad."

"See you tomorrow, Debra."

Dad left, and I sat beside Mom's bed. She had bruises covering half her arm. I wanted to hold her hand, but she had an IV in it.

"They did a goddamn bone marrow test this afternoon. Hurt like hell. I don't know what the fuck that was all about." She sighed and shook her head. "I'm sorry I'm cursing. I know I shouldn't make things any harder on you. I just don't feel good."

"It's okay, Mom. You've got more important things to worry about."

"But I should be stronger." She looked at her hands and suddenly got a disgusted look on her face.

We didn't talk much over the next few hours. The TV was on, and Mom watched it intently, the look on her face now an angry one. I'd brought my Western Civilization notebook and studied a bit out of that, a little uncomfortable.

Around 8:00, the doctor came by and made Mom stand up beside the bed and walk a few steps. Mom swore, but she did it.

"We'll have you walking down the hall tomorrow," said the doctor, smiling despite my mom's scowl. "And you'll be home tomorrow night."

Mom was indeed home by the next evening. She still didn't feel very good and went straight to bed. I left her alone but thought about her while delivering pizza in the rain later. The next day was Sunday, so after church, I went in to sit on Mom's bed beside her. "All those bruises look painful," I said in a worried tone. Then I added impishly, "Maybe we should try some acupuncture to relieve the pain."

She smiled for the first time in days. "I think acupuncture is what caused all the bruises in the first place."

We chatted for an hour, and then she got a call from the Relief Society president, so I left her alone then. She looked like she'd be back to normal soon. I checked on her just once more a couple of hours later, and since it was Sunday, I asked if she wanted me to bring her scriptures to her. She nodded absently, but when I handed her the Book of Mormon, she looked at the cover for a long moment and then put the book aside.

Because it was the Sabbath, I didn't study for school. Instead, I emailed some friends in Bucharest and my aunt Robin in Jackson. Then I read some of *Faith Precedes the Miracle*, and a little of *Life After Life*, about near death experiences.

Mom came down for breakfast the next morning, and Dad cooked for her. I had a bowl of cereal and headed off to school. Mom was back in bed resting when I got home in the late afternoon. Dad fixed Mom some soup, and I had a sandwich.

Then I headed over to the stake president's house. Their oldest daughter was hosting the Single Adult Family Home Evening. We had a brief lesson on charity and then played Truth or Dare. For one of my truths, I had to reveal my first crush, which was easy enough—it was my first grade teacher, Miss Kavanaugh. At least they didn't ask for my second crush, which would have been Mr. Edwards, in second grade. Or my third, which would have been Coach Marks in 8th grade. Or my fourth, which would have been my classmate Jim in 9th grade. Or my fifth…

As much as I had to hide, I still always chose Truth in Truth or Dare. I was too wimpy to ever do a Dare.

The stake president, who'd left the Single Adults alone during the evening, came up to me at the end of the meeting. "Your Dad just called. He had to take your mom back to the hospital. She has a high fever. She's in East Jefferson."

"I'd better stop by on my way home."

He put his hand on my shoulder. "If you were my son, you'd be working your way through college. I don't approve of your dad paying your way. I'd teach you some responsibility. I'd make a man out of you."

My first impulse was to say, "Thank God you're not my dad." But I knew my father and President Brooks were friends, so I just smiled and left. I couldn't help but notice he didn't have any problem paying his daughter's way through college.

On my way to the hospital, though, I thought about what the stake president had said. Would it make me a better person to move out on my own and get a full-time job and just go to school part-time? I was two years behind most of my classmates as it was, but was that as important as being self-sufficient? I could get student loans and be $50,000 in debt by the time I finished school. It would be a hard way to start my adult life, but hard wasn't necessarily bad.

But so what if I was a lazy bum for staying at home while going to school? I was going to hell anyway. Why did I need to bother with improving my character? I was studying hard and getting A's, taking five classes a semester. I didn't date or go out or waste the money my dad gave me at the beginning of each semester. I might be wickedly evil, but I was nevertheless a good kid.

Yet I was still a kid. Even after a two-year mission. Even after going through the temple. Even after a year and a half of college. I was still just a kid.

When I got to the hospital, I went up to my mom's room. I wondered if the fact that she was in a larger hospital this time meant the infection that had caused her fever was serious. I offered up a quick prayer, put a smile on my face, and went into my mom's room. My dad was sitting next to the bed.

"I want to talk to Gary alone for a minute," said my mom curtly, and Dad nodded tand left the room.

I took my dad's place in the chair and held my mom's hand.

"I am super pissed off," she said. "Do you know when they were admitting me, the nurse looked at my chart and said, 'Oh, you're the leukemia patient.' So that's how I found out I have leukemia."

"You have leukemia?"

"Your dad wasn't going to tell me. He thinks I'm too fragile. But I can tell you this—if I'd known what I had, I'd have stayed at home and blown my brains out. But now I'm trapped here, on chemotherapy, and I can't get out. My whole life, people have been telling me what to do. Even now, I don't have any say over my own life. I am really pissed."

My mind was going a mile a minute, but mostly I was thinking maybe my dad was right not to tell her, if it kept her from committing suicide. The Church said that was a terrible sin. There was no sense going to hell when you were so close to finishing your test.

But certainly she wasn't about to "finish." She wasn't going to die. The chemotherapy was going to work. Certainly it would. There were huge strides forward in cancer treatment all the time. And this was my mom. My mom couldn't possibly die. Those things only happened to other people.

My mom grasped my hand. "They won't tell me my prognosis. But I got them to tell me the name of the leukemia. It's acute lymphatic leukemia. I want you to go to the library and find out how long I've got."

"Okay," I said numbly.

She squeezed my hand harder. "I just want you to know," she said, looking at me intently, "that I've always loved you. I've always been proud of you. I couldn't have had a better son."

"There's no need to talk like that, Mom. You're not going anywhere."

"We'll see. You come back and tell me my prognosis tomorrow."

"Okay."

"And for God's sake, don't let the Relief Society president come. I can't stand that bitch. I don't feel like pretending I like her at a time like this. I don't have the patience for all that trash. And I'm not going to apologize for it, either."

"I'll call and tell her you're not up to having visitors."

"Hell, you can tell her the truth for all I care. I'm sick of pretending." She laughed a little bitterly. "Maybe I'm sick *from* pretending."

I nodded, knowing I'd of course want to find something diplomatic to say. I'd been voted Most Courteous in high school. With so many defects in my character, being nice was one of the very few things I had going for me. But was there really any pressing reason to be nice, I wondered, if I was going to hell anyway?

"Call your aunt Robin and ask her to come down. I want to see her before I die."

"You're not going to die."

"I want to see her. And call Grandma, too."

"I'll call them tonight."

Grandma drove a couple of hours down from Brookhaven the next morning, and Robin left her two teens and husband home in Jackson and came down early in the afternoon, before I was back again after school.

"What's the verdict?" Mom demanded as soon as I walked into the room. Three pairs of eyes stared intensely at me.

"If the chemotherapy doesn't work," I began uncomfortably, "you have about three months."

My mom deflated in front of me like a punctured balloon, and I felt like a murderer. I didn't have the heart to go on, to say that even with successful chemotherapy, which was rare, remission usually only lasted a single year. All our worlds were being turned upside down.

Mom didn't say anything more the rest of the afternoon, other than muttering "shit" a couple of times. Robin and Grandma tried to carry on a cheerful conversation, but Mom took no part in it, and I didn't, either. Around 9:30, Dad came to stay with Mom for the night, and the three of us went back to the house.

"The chemotherapy will get rid of the bad cells," said Robin as we came inside. "It's all going to work out fine.

Tomorrow morning before you go to school, you and your dad need to give your mom a blessing. You still carry your consecrated oil with you, don't you?"

"Yes."

"Then everything is going to be all right."

Grandma looked unconvinced but smiled weakly, yet I knew that God would never honor a blessing made by a homosexual, even though I was still a virgin. I wasn't a virgin in my thoughts, of course, and I knew God hated me for it. He'd certainly never save my mom on my account. Maybe I could get the bishop to do the blessing with Dad.

I went upstairs and called Bishop Tillotson, asking if he could stop by the hospital in the morning before he went to work. He agreed, and I sighed in relief.

The hospital was on my way to school, so I dropped Robin and Grandma off in the morning. Dad looked beat but said he and the bishop had given Mom a blessing earlier. I looked at Mom as he told me this, and she was glaring at Dad.

I was through with classes by 3:00 and went back to the hospital. A nurse came into the room to draw blood, but Mom's arms were already covered with bruises. A little later, I noticed that the tubing had become disconnected to the IV in her hand. I pushed the call button, and about five minutes later a nurse responded. I explained what had occurred, and the nurse angrily told me that this couldn't happen. I insisted she come look, and the nurse came several minutes later. When she saw the tubing, she didn't say anything but just reattached the hose and left, still angry. For some reason, I felt guilty.

The next few days went by in much the same manner. Robin and Grandma did the mornings. I came in mid-afternoon, took them home, and went back till the late evening. Dad came around 10:00 and stayed the night.

Mom didn't talk much, so on my shifts, I mostly studied or told Mom stories of my mission experiences in Romania. I'd had a favorite companion, Nicolae Petrescu, who'd just written me a long email, so I told her what he was up to these days. She didn't look overly interested, but I felt we had to talk about something. I didn't tell her that Nicolae had said he missed me. "Mi-e dor de tine!" he'd said, I remembered now, smiling.

I asked if she wanted me to bring her a book to read. She had probably two thousand books at the house and particularly loved mysteries, though I had found a few classics and also a few books about sex on her shelves, too. She had a locked cabinet in her tiny study, and she had never let anyone see what was inside. She had collected first editions for a while, and I figured she kept a few rare books in there. Perhaps if I brought her something special from home, she'd feel a little better.

"My reading days are over," she said. "Take whatever books you want, and get rid of the rest. And don't clutter up your house with all that junk like I did mine. Use the library."

"But you love your books, Mom. There's no sin in enjoying something."

She stared at the ceiling. "I wish I had actually done something with my life." I put my hand lightly on her arm, afraid of hurting her. "I wasted all that time being a good little girl. God, I wish I'd posed for *Playboy* or something when I was young. Or gone to college myself. Or written something. Or backpacked across Europe. Or gotten arrested. I wish I'd done something interesting."

"You got married in the temple and raised a family." I felt stupid saying it, knowing that forced her to say she was glad she'd had me.

"Having a kid shouldn't mean you never get to do anything else interesting with your life."

"No," I agreed. "You're right."

Unfortunately, our talks tapered off quickly after this. By the next day, Mom was starting to lose her sense of awareness of what was going on around her. Once, after a nurse left, Mom asked me, "Who was that?"

"The nurse."

"Should we help her?"

"She doesn't need any help."

"Why not? Did we already help her?"

I nodded. "Yes, we helped her." I thought that should end the discussion, but my mom looked confused.

"What did we do?"

I didn't know what to say at this point. "You gave her some blood." Mom just looked at me like I was crazy.

The next few days were worse. One morning, I stopped in to see her briefly while dropping Robin and Grandma off, and two nurses were lifting Mom in a huge sling so they could weigh her, since she couldn't stand to get on a scale. They had to push her over to one side to slide the fabric under her, and then push her over to the other side to pull it the rest of the way across. It was clear they were hurting her, and I wondered how knowing if she'd lost or gained a pound could possibly be so important.

After the nurses finally left, Mom turned to me and said encouragingly, "Gary, you can get your snakes now."

I smiled and thanked her.

Another time, in the afternoon, I watched as a nurse poked my mom's almost entirely blue arm to draw yet more blood. After the nurse left, my mom turned to me with a completely disgusted look on her face. "Why did we join this club?" she asked miserably.

That evening, Dad came a half hour early to relieve me. "Gary, I had to revise my proposal for the job. Would you mind retyping it before bed tonight?"

"Sure, Dad. But you didn't have to get here early for that. I can stay up a little later."

"It's okay, son."

I'd taken a couple more exams at school and was still doing okay. I felt I had to prove to God that I could take the stress and still perform, that doing well while my mom was sick was a test He was giving me, that perhaps it would somehow change my soul. I thought about what my mom had said. We had joined the "club" of Earth life so we could pass the tests God gave us and become gods. It was a miserable club sometimes, but if we could do well even at the worst of times, it would all pay off in the end. I wondered, though, what it would be like to take a class just for the sake of learning, not as a method of proving myself. What would it be like just to enjoy life for the sake of living, and not as part of creating a celestial resume'?

I retyped Dad's proposal and read a few more pages of my Book of Mormon in Romanian, and then I went to bed.

The next afternoon when I walked into Mom's room after dropping Robin and Grandma off at the house, two nurses met me at the door. "We have to draw so much blood, and we're running out of veins, so we decided to put this tube inside her arm, and now we can always just stick a needle into the tube."

I was irritated that they hadn't thought of that right at the beginning. Did they not know in advance they'd be using up all her veins? I almost said something, but then I thought I ought to be polite.

I sat off to the side and watched as the nurses cut and dug into my Mom's arm. Mom grunted and cried, and I squirmed in my chair. But if they could do this, it would lessen the suffering later. The nurses kept working and shoving and muttering, and my mom kept crying and moaning. It went on and on and on. After fifteen horrendous minutes, I couldn't take it anymore and left the room.

But the nurses didn't come out for yet another fifteen minutes. Half an hour of sheer, literal torture. But at least it was done. I felt ashamed for leaving Mom alone during all of that, but relieved it was over.

"So the tube is in?" I asked.

"No, we didn't get it," one of the nurses said. "Her veins are too damaged. We couldn't get rid of all the clogs." She shrugged and walked off, unconcerned, and I had to fight not to hit her.

The next day was even worse. When I arrived to pick up Robin and Grandma, Mom was sleeping, but a nurse came in to draw more blood, and Mom woke up moaning from the pain. She'd always had veins that were hard to find anyway, and now the nurses had to dig and dig.

While the nurse was digging in my mom's leg, Mom began looking around wildly, her eyes searching desperately and blindly for help, and then she threw her arms up to the ceiling and wailed, "I want my Mama!"

Grandma sobbed loudly and rushed over to her, but Mom seemed not to recognize her. She cried as the nurse continued to work on her, and Grandma cried, and Robin cried, and I thought life could never get any worse than this.

But it did. The next morning, Dad reported that he'd been up all night, that Mom was now bleeding from her bowels, and he'd had to empty the bedpan every twenty minutes. Mom's platelets were gone, and she wasn't reacting well to the platelet transfusions.

He stayed a little longer so Robin and Grandma could do platelet pheresis, in the hopes that Mom wouldn't reject her family's platelets, and I went right after school to have my platelets taken out, too. It took about 90 minutes, a nurse taking blood out of one arm, spinning it in a centrifuge, scooping out the layer of platelets, and putting the rest of the blood back in the other arm, repeating the process over and over.

So I didn't get to Mom's room till around 5:00. I called Dad to tell him not to come till he'd taken a long nap, that I could do more than just five hours for my shift, since I knew I always had the shortest shift of anyone in the family to begin with.

Dad came at 11:00, though, and with my emptying the bedpan every twenty or thirty minutes, even those six hours seemed an eternity. But Dad's shift was even longer, and he was trying to maintain a business as well. I wondered if I should drop out of school and carry more of the burden. But there was only a month left to the semester. It seemed like such a waste to just chuck two and a half months of work. And maybe managing all of it together really would help God to bless me. If my dad could handle his heavy load, surely I could handle this little one. And maybe the blessing that this might bring would be an improvement in Mom's health rather than an improvement in my soul. Maybe it would be an improvement in my mom's soul instead, a reconversion to the gospel. This illness seemed like the "trial of her faith," and I was afraid she was losing her testimony. I had started fasting every other day, asking God to save my mom's life or her soul, whichever He had more power to do.

I hardly had any interaction with anyone at all these days, studying non-stop between classes, driving my car delivering pizza on weekends, and spending just a few minutes with my family during shift changes. Mom slept or moaned or talked crazy while I was with her. I wasn't sure she could even regain her testimony now in any event if she was no longer lucid. So I hoped the chemotherapy would work long enough to let her be happy with her gospel-centered life.

The Relief Society president insisted on coming over one evening despite what I'd told her, but Mom didn't seem to notice. A couple of other members of the ward came by on other days, but really, Mom had never made many friends over the years, keeping to herself a lot, so no one seemed to really care that she was sick besides us. It struck me that completely devoting yourself to your family must be a limiting, lonely life, no matter how righteous. Maybe there really was something to be sorry about in that. Perhaps Mom wasn't losing her testimony now so much as repenting.

One day, though, without warning, Mom looked at me and seemed to be her old self again. It was like a miracle, and I smiled to see the recognition in her eyes. "You're getting better," I said.

"It would have been so much better still if I'd just shot myself."

I wondered then if she might be right, but I said, "The chemotherapy's working, and you're going to be fine." Then I had a horrible thought—what if in fact the chemotherapy *did* work, and she went into remission, and then a year from now had to die all over again? I suddenly hoped the treatments wouldn't work. Dying once was bad enough.

"Don't waste your life like I did," Mom said. "Time isn't something to be tossed away like so much garbage."

"You didn't waste your life, Mom. You read me stories. You made peanut butter fudge for Christmas. You went to the Smoky Mountains with Dad every year."

"I'm 43, and I only had about ten good years out of that."

"You went to the temple. You taught Relief Society. Didn't you enjoy any of that?" How could she not have felt the Spirit and liked it?

Mom sighed. "So much time wasted doing what I was supposed to do."

"Well, if we're supposed to do it…"

"The Church gives us materials to build our lives. I know. But sometimes even good things become scrap."

"Your life isn't scrap."

She smiled weakly. "I meant the building materials."

"But the Church helps us so much."

"My only hope is to be myself the little time I have left." Her eyes narrowed as she looked straight ahead.

"We have all eternity, Mom. Even if you die, it's not the end."

She looked at me sadly. "You need to find yourself a nice young man," she said softly. "Maybe this guy Nicolae you like so much."

"What?"

"Don't throw away your whole life. If there really is something beyond all this, what we get will depend on how well we used what we were given here. Being nice and following the rules isn't the most important thing in the world. Live while you're alive. God, the things I wanted to do. The things I meant to do." She looked at the IV pole sadly. "The things I'll never do."

She seemed exhausted after this and closed her eyes. I looked at her and realized I was tightly clutching the sheet on the bed. My mind was reeling from the discovery that my mom had known I was gay all along. But living in the Church, of course, was the only real way to have happiness in the next world. She was wrong to be upset that she'd been "good" all her life.

Yet somehow, her words seemed just as valid as any scripture I'd ever read. However many "near death" experiences were out there, I'd certainly never talked to anyone who'd been on the other side. Talking to someone this near to death was as close as I was likely to get, and it seemed to make her more of an authority, though maybe it was only an apparent lucidity and she was still talking crazy.

I was wondering what else to ask her while she was still reasonably coherent, but suddenly her eyes rolled up and she began shaking. The whole bed started rocking. I didn't bother with the call button but ran to the door and shouted for help.

The convulsions were over in a few minutes, but when the doctor came later, he said she'd had a stroke. It was too early to tell if there would be permanent damage or not.

The doctor left, and after I emptied the bedpan again, wiped Mom's legs, and tried to shove some clean pads underneath her, I sat with my head in my hands. Was Mom being punished for her heresy? Or was this a blessing, to knock her out so she wouldn't feel so much pain? Or to keep her from sinning even more?

I hesitated to call my dad but felt he'd want to know, and he came to the hospital by 9:00. I stayed with him a while longer, but neither of us said anything. Then I went home.

I had an Italian test the next day. I'd picked Italian to fulfill my language requirement since it was the closest thing offered to Romanian. My heart wasn't in it today, but I forced myself to concentrate and was sure I'd made an A.

To my great surprise, my mom was awake when I got back to the hospital. There seemed to be no lasting effects from the stroke. It was another miracle. Maybe that meant

God really was going to bless her. I rushed back after dropping Robin and Grandma off at the house.

"I'm afraid I've been too protective of you," Mom said sadly as I held her hand. "God is getting rid of me so you can grow up."

"If I'm immature, that's my problem," I said. "God doesn't impose the death penalty for a thing like that."

She just shook her head in a melancholy way and smiled weakly. Then I emptied her bedpan again.

Mom talked about growing up in the country in Mississippi, finding arrowheads in the pasture behind her house, the big day when the gravel road out front was finally paved, and the day her parents met two Mormon missionaries in town. I realized we'd never talked as adults before, and I suddenly wanted desperately for her to survive so I could finally get to know her as a person.

"You know, Gary," she said then, "the Church thinks you're trash. They'll try to get rid of you." She patted my hand, her IV tube glistening in the light. "But that's okay. I worried about it for a while." She stopped, and her face grew harder. "But you don't need to carry all that baggage around with you the rest of your life, like I did. Guilt and fear are pretty useless emotions." She paused and then added uncertainly, "Do you think Nicolae might really like you? You know, the way you like him?"

I felt my face flush. It was just too strange to be talking like this. How could my mom be so calm? "I—I don't know," I said. "I hope so." I felt I was going to be struck down with leukemia, too, for saying it.

She nodded. "Then you'll get a job this summer and save up some money to go see him. Or you'll invite him here to stay with you a few weeks to find out."

"Okay," I mumbled, my ears and cheeks still burning.

"These things don't happen on their own. You have to make them happen. If you don't, your whole life goes by without anything good ever getting done."

I was looking down at the floor, too embarrassed to look my mom in the face. She put her hand on my arm. "I suppose everyone looks for meaning at a shitty time like this. But if I can just teach you not to treat your chances like junk, maybe my life would have been worth it." She paused and then managed a brief smile. "God, it feels good to finally say all these things I've been thinking for so many years." She laughed a little. "I'm still a Stepford wife when your dad comes in the evening. No sense upsetting him. Maybe you can never truly be the person you want to be completely. You always have to worry about how others are going to be affected. But Gary, don't worry about it as much as I did."

We talked about other things then, me just enjoying her company. She *was* more fun like this, more interesting, more real. I felt mystified and guilty that I even thought the word "fun" in such circumstances. I always felt like my mom and I had been close, but the definition of "close" had changed in the past few days. I could see how robotic I'd been myself as a missionary, how robotic I was now in church. As much as I loved Nicolae, how often had we ever actually talked about anything that mattered to us outside of religion? Was I up to spending the next twenty years just writing him about how things were going in the ward and hoping the work was going well over in Romania? Never telling him anything deeper I was feeling?

Mom whispered to me where she kept her dildo and told me to find it before my dad did. I didn't even know what she was talking about until she explained it. Two weeks ago, I would have been mortified, but now I just nodded and assured her I'd take care of it. I turned the nurse away once when she came to draw blood. The woman was angry, but she left. Then Mom and I talked about how I would need to help Dad by taking over the cooking and cleaning, how I would give Mom's clothes to some of the poorer members of the congregation, how I was to keep no more than a hundred of Mom's books and then donate the rest to the public library, and how I was to be sure to visit Grandma often and be a support to her. Robin was to have the one painting Mom had done, of their childhood home in Mississippi. I was to be nice to whatever woman my dad eventually chose to marry.

Mom was very calm but firm about everything. I felt selfish, spending all this special time alone with her while everyone else was away. But maybe she'd talked to them this way, too. I hoped so.

I emptied the bedpan a few more times. Mom always moaned when I turned her over, and around 8:30, when I pushed her back into place, after another bedpan moment, she had a glazed look on her face. "Why is it raining in here?" she asked in alarm. "Get rid of those dogs!"

It had happened so suddenly, I didn't know what to do. Then in a matter of seconds, her eyes rolled up, and her jaw clenched tight, and she started shaking again. There was nothing to be done, so I didn't feel a sense of urgency. I calmly pressed the call button and told the nurse what was happening.

The seizure was over in a couple of minutes, but by the time the doctor arrived an hour later, things seemed pretty grim. "You can see by the way she's holding her hand that she's had a severe stroke. I expect she's paralyzed on her left side. It's impossible to tell right now how much of her brain function is left, but it doesn't look good. The other tests show her kidneys are shutting down, too, and it looks like she may be developing diabetes."

Dad was due in a few minutes, but I didn't want him to feel neglected, so I called and told him what had happened. When I saw him looking down at Mom a few minutes later, I could see that he'd finally given up. I knew he wouldn't like my doing it, but I went over and hugged him anyway. He was unresponsive at first but eventually started hugging me back. Then he released me and said, "You go get some sleep, son."

The next morning, Dad didn't leave when I brought Robin and Grandma. I thought maybe I should skip school for just one day, since Mom might die at any moment, but I had a geology test, and I didn't want to have to reschedule. Would Mom have wanted me to be just a little selfish instead of doing the respectable thing? It was probably just rationalization. I wasn't able to put Mom out of my mind during the test, but I found I could think of her and still concentrate on continental drift at the same time. It somehow made me realize that life truly was a test, whether God was behind it or not, and some days there was going to be more than one test at a time.

I arrived back at the hospital a few minutes after 3:00. Dad, Robin, and Grandma were in the hall outside Mom's door. They all looked exhausted.

Dad came up to me and grabbed my arm. "Your Mom died five minutes ago."

My first reaction was to feel a wave of guilt. I wasn't there when my mother died. Had I let a stupid class be more important to me? But immediately afterward, I thought, "If God had wanted me to be there, He could have kept her alive five extra minutes."

"I want to see her."

I went in the room and looked at her motionless body. It was clearly just an empty shell now. Then I looked up at the ceiling, and into the corners. Was she up there right now looking down at me? Or had she gone on to meet her father and grandparents?

Would she have fun in the next world, I wondered. Would there still be books to read? Would she have a chance to write one of her own? Or to pose nude for someone? Was there "spirit body" porn? Would she have a chance to finally make some friends? Or to do any of the things she'd missed out on here?

There was an eternity ahead of her. Surely, God wouldn't condemn her completely for all of forever just for whatever few mistakes she'd made here.

But I wasn't going to take a chance.

Robin, Grandma, and I went back to the house while Dad stayed at the hospital to make arrangements. As soon as we closed the door behind us, our Chihuahua started pawing frantically at the carpet in front of the door, trying to get out. She knew Mom wasn't coming back. I picked her up and held her, and she squealed pitifully. She howled for fifteen minutes, and I held her the entire time. But when Dad got home later, I had dinner ready for everyone. Even Robin and Grandma hadn't felt like cooking.

But after dinner and a little subdued conversation, I went up to my room, and I chucked out my copy of *The Miracle of Forgiveness* with its homophobic chapter on homosexuality. I looked online for gay support groups in New Orleans and found a chapter of PFLAG that met once a month, with a meeting to be held just next week. And then I emailed Nicolae, telling him about the last few weeks, and asking if he was up for a visit from me in August.

It was only November, so a full-time summer job was months away, but I started looking for another part-time job right now. Maybe I could tutor ESL students at school and work toward a degree in that field so I could get a job in Romania teaching English.

Maybe Nicolae would rather move to America, though. Or maybe he didn't really like me the same way I liked him in the first place. But whatever happened, I was going to try to do something interesting with my life. Maybe I'd pose for a magazine myself one day. I was already in good shape, but I did some push ups and sit ups for a while as I thought about it, and then I studied a little more of Shakespeare.

After I felt I'd done as much as I could for the evening, I got out my photo album and began looking through all my pictures. I was shocked to find I'd only taken six photos of my mom in 21 years. The last one I had taken was over a year before my mission. How could that have happened?

In two days, the person who meant most to me in my life would be taken away and buried like so much garbage in a landfill. But I was going to make her life mean something. I was going to make my own life mean something, too. I'd make sure I had something interesting to tell her the next time we met. She'd said she was proud of me, but I'd make sure I would make her even prouder. Maybe God wouldn't think much of me, but my mom would.

One thing was for sure--I wasn't going to let the Relief Society president say anything at the service.

I looked at the old photo of my mom and gently caressed it, and then I kissed her goodbye.

The Hotel Room

"Don't think I don't know what you're doing," said Sefton when I'd finished. "I'm not stupid."

"What do you mean?" I asked in my most innocent voice.

"You know more about Mormons than you're letting on. This isn't all from some conversation you had with your boyfriend over dinner."

I smiled and shrugged. "Yes, I'm Mormon, too, so I understand where you're coming from."

"You're nothing like me. I'm staying true to the Gospel."

Oh, brother. This is why I hadn't wanted to tell him. But I could hardly keep the pretense up all night. "I heard a lot of stories similar to ours when I belonged to Affirmation."

"Those guys are apostates," Sefton said flatly.

"Who cares?" I said. "I'm not trying to convert you. Everything doesn't have to be about conversion. I'm just trying to tell you a good story."

"Well, if that's your goal, the trick is not to tell me the ending. That way I'll stay longer. But you keep telling me the ending of each story, so I can leave at any point. And I think it's time you put on your clothes."

"Sure, Sefton," I said agreeably, making no effort to pick up even a single piece of clothing. "But did you ever hear the one about—"

"Nice try," he said. "But why bother? Even if this bill doesn't pass, there will be another. Maybe it'll be one to limit immigration for gays. Or maybe it'll be one that says a gay couple can't adopt if one of the partners is non-U.S. born. Perhaps it'll be one to ban gay elementary school teachers. Or even one as outrageous as to ban gays from owning guns, because they're an oppressed minority and might have more reason to use them."

"They're oppressed, which makes them dangerous, so let's oppress them some more?" I said with a grim smile.

"It could be anything," Sefton went on. "You see how it is with abortion. It's a Constitutionally-guaranteed right, but we find ways to chip away at it every day. Rightfully so, of course. And it'll be the same with gays. You can't win."

I put my hand around Sefton's penis, which was stiffening again. I wondered if anger had made him hard. Still, I enjoyed feeling his cock throb under my fingers. Sefton wasn't a bad looking man, perhaps a few years older than the guys I usually went out with. But I could see myself going home with him willingly from a bar or a party.

On a regular date, however, I would simply have to gag him to keep him from making so many homophobic comments.

"Well, if it's a foregone conclusion," I said, "then there's no reason we can't keep talking." Though I really wanted to gag him right now, too. And I knew just what to do it with. "I think we've rested enough that we can make another go at it. Is there anything you'd like to do we didn't do last time? I'm pretty versatile in almost every way." I climbed on top of Sefton before he could protest and put my lips against his. He resisted for just a moment, and then his lips parted, and he welcomed my tongue.

Usually, the second round of sex goes more quickly than the first round, but almost fifty minutes passed before we finished, spent and depleted. I knew I could easily charge Sefton twice, but I had no intention of trying to gouge him financially. We lay next to each other afterward, just as we had the first time, my head on Sefton's chest. He caressed my back softly and actually purred for a moment.

"So tell me another story," he said.

He couldn't see my grin, but I was sure he heard it in my voice as I began.

Bus Surfing

"Come on, it's 3:30," I said to Elder Deiana, picking up my notebook and Bible. "You ready, Anziano?"

"Si'," he replied, but headed for the bathroom to brush his teeth. I smiled and opened my notebook, studying the crude map I had drawn a couple of weeks earlier. Elder Deiana and I had tracted out almost half the streets in our new tracting zone in northeastern Rome, no small feat considering that nearly every apartment building was seven or eight stories high. Several doormen, however, had "helped" us speed along in our zone by refusing to let us tract out their buildings. Some wouldn't even allow us to use the citofono, or intercom, outside.

Deiana was pretty good with portieri, though. We were able to sneak past a few each night, and if we got caught, he could usually laugh or talk his way out of a potentially sticky situation. "Oh, I'm sorry," he'd say. "We didn't see you sitting right there in your desk by the door." The portieri were never pleased, but my companion's obvious lie and the twinkle in his eyes would usually get us off the hook without being shouted at too loudly.

Elder Deiana glided into the room then, showing me his clean teeth in a wide grin. He picked up a Book of Mormon and a few pamphlets from off of his desk. "Ready?" he inquired innocently.

After Deiana offered a brief prayer, we headed out of the apartment and down the street toward the bus stop. It was annoying to have to run half a block right after lunch to catch a bus, so we walked quickly down Via Franco Sacchetti and hoped we would be close to the bus stop if the bus suddenly turned the corner. Just yesterday, we'd had to race for the bus, but Deiana had had to pause to avoid being hit by a car. I didn't realize he wasn't right behind me until the bus took off and I saw him waving at me. I'd stepped off the bus at the next stop and walked back to my companion. We'd had to wait another fifteen minutes for the next bus.

Resting at the bus stop now, I glanced at Elder Deiana. He was a few inches shorter than I was, about 5' 6", with short, straight black hair and olive skin, wearing a stylish Italian suit compared to my cheap American one. He was looking at a pretty, dark-haired girl who was reading a book. Deiana was always pointing out girls reading books. "Antonella read that one, too," he'd say, or "Antonella told me that one was garbage." I'd heard enough praise of Antonella to expect her to be swept up in a chariot of fire. "I like a girl who takes care of her body," explained Deiana, "but she's also got to use her mind."

A girl's mind was about all I cared about when meeting the girl, and I liked that Deiana at least put that somewhere on his list of priorities. I wondered if he'd find me attractive if I was a girl, but I had no desire to be a girl, and I didn't want Deiana to be one, either. I liked him as he was.

I had never told anyone about liking guys, and I'd hoped two years as a missionary would purge those sinful feelings out of me, make me worth liking as a person. The feelings were still there, though, and I didn't know what I was going to do about them, but I was sure that God had had a purpose in mind when he'd given me a companion I could really love. Maybe being with Deiana would satisfy that need I had to have at least one man love me during my life.

I looked over at Deiana again. He had a contented grin as he continued to look at the young woman reading her novel. Deiana always smiled when he saw a girl reading a book. He seemed to be sentimental about a lot of things. So was I. I think that's why I dreaded the next day so much. Transfers. Deiana and I had already been together for two months in the Rome Four district, and I had never stayed with a companion for longer than that. It was almost certain that one of us would be leaving in two days.

It seemed as if those two months had flown by, but I could hardly remember a time without Deiana. We had done so much together. Friendships usually came and went with transfers, but Deiana and I shared something special. We weren't just compatible companions. We were friends and really cared about each other, especially when we could sense that the other was discouraged or feeling depressed about something. Like that time I had cooked eggs and potatoes for Deiana one morning, the day after he'd received his "Dear John" from Antonella. Or the time he had washed the dishes for me one afternoon when it was my turn. I had been discouraged with our lack of success in the work, and I felt like a failure. But I decided that if Deiana thought enough of me to help me out, I must have something going for me. I hadn't made many friends back in America, and I certainly hadn't made many out here. It was refreshing to have someone sincerely care about me now. Especially another man.

I had felt reasonably close to a couple of other companions previously. Nothing too special, but I would have liked to keep in touch after we'd been transferred apart. It was against mission rules to write letters within mission boundaries, though, so when transfers had come, that was that. Maybe we'd see each other again at a zone conference or something, and maybe not. Would I break that rule for Deiana, though, and keep in touch after transfers? Would he be willing to break it as well?

"Anziano Anderson," my companion interrupted my thoughts. "Here comes the bus." We crowded in behind the other passengers. Since we didn't have to worry about tickets, having bought a monthly pass for eight thousand lire, we squeezed by some of the other passengers and made our way to a reasonably vacant spot near the front of the bus, where we grasped a metal bar above our heads as the bus took off.

Sometimes, we talked to the other passengers, trying to get their addresses so we could go teach them, but usually my companion and I just talked to each other. It had been during our on-bus conversations that I had learned a lot about Deiana's past. Almost every time we passed the army outpost on Via Nomentana, I heard another story of the year Deiana spent as an Italian paratrooper. Even though his service had been obligatory and difficult in many ways (hassles with leaders and rules, mostly—Deiana sometimes had a big mouth), he seemed to enjoy a lot of the things he'd had to do that year. He told me of the times he and his buddies had clogged the bathroom drains in the barracks and had slid naked on their stomachs in the three-inch deep water on the floor, and about how they would terrorize the new "allievi" in the middle of the night by making them leap off of upper bunks in the dark onto mattresses they couldn't see. He reminisced about using the big guns on the base and the war games they played. Once, due to a miscalculation, a huge shell from the opposing team had landed almost at his feet. Fortunately, the ground was wet from rain and the shell had sunk about ten feet before exploding.

One day last week after relating one of these stories to me, he'd paused, fingered his dog tag which he still liked to wear almost every day, and had then handed the tag to me nonchalantly, but had quickly turned to talk to a nearby man about the Church before I could say anything. Now I wore it every day. Another time when I'd asked about parachuting, he'd told me, "I was scared to death to jump out of that first plane, but since I had to go, I decided I might as well take a picture of myself falling," and he'd given me a copy of that picture later.

It was also on the way to our tracting zone near Piazza Bologna where I learned about some of Deiana's hobbies. He liked mountain climbing in the Alps, north of his home in Milano, and he enjoyed camping. I was surprised to find that I was interested to hear him talk about his hobbies because I had little desire to participate in them, though I had to admit that his example with weightlifting had gotten me to work out with him twice a week so far. And his soccer lessons each Preparation Day had made the game at least reasonably fun for me, though I had never been much into sports before.

More than that, though, I think we discovered that we were both simply nice, that because we never tried to take advantage of each other or insist on having our own way, that it was a pleasure to be together. Once, Elder Lucas, our zone leader, had ordered a "work visit" with Deiana, intending to take my place as companion for an evening. But while Lucas was brushing his teeth after lunch, Deiana had pointed silently to the door and led me outside so he could work with me instead. "You're my companion," he'd said, giving me a light kiss on the forehead. "I want to work with *you*."

"Our stop's next," Deiana said, pushing a square red button near a window. We edged over to the two doors near the center of the bus. When the bus stopped, we jumped down and crossed over to Viale XXI Aprile. We usually had to wait for the light, but our timing was just right this time. We passed the blue and white police van, always parked in the same place, and about seven young policemen.

We had been right there by that police van when Deiana told me about the time he was in Milano on his way to school one morning and saw a carabiniere get shot to death by the Red Brigade. The carabiniere had been just a young man serving his obligatory military term, but had had the misfortune of standing next to a higher officer, who had been seriously wounded in the incident. I think it was also as we passed the van, but on our way home one night, when Deiana reminisced about the fights he and his friends in the military used to get in with the local punks in Livorno, where they were stationed, and about the time he was beaten in Milano after refusing to give up his wallet to a couple of thugs. He lost his wallet, anyway, but he said he always loved a good fight.

A few minutes later, we were on Via Pisa, so I opened my notebook and checked to see where the next building we needed to tract out would be. We had to walk about two thirds of the way down the street before we could start tracting. We walked over to the next building on our list, went into the elevator, and pushed 7. At least we didn't have to pay ten lire each trip up, like down in Napoli. Most of the elevators in Rome were free.

"You're awfully quiet tonight, Elder," Deiana told me as we got out of the elevator on the top floor. "Anything wrong?"

"Oh, just thinking a little. It wears me out," I replied, smiling.

"I can understand that." He smiled back and pushed the doorbell of the first door.

A moment later, the door opened. A middle-aged woman answered. "Chi e'?"

"Good evening. We're two representatives of The Church of Jesus Christ of Latter-day Saints, and we have a short message we'd like to share with you and your family." Elder Deiana paused. "Is your husband in?"

"No." She closed the door.

"Oh, well. Good evening," he replied.

"Not your type, Elder." I pushed the next doorbell. "What is your type, anyway?" I wondered if his type had changed any since Antonella.

"Can I give a long answer?" He laughed.

"Sure."

"Well, she'd have to be pretty, have auburn hair—"

"Auburn?"

"Uh-huh, and be fun."

I pushed the doorbell again. I wasn't sure if I heard anything, so I knocked. "What do you mean by 'fun'?"

"Oh, you know. Crazy. We can joke and laugh and have fun."

"Oh." We started down the stairs.

"But," he added, "she has to be serious at the right times."

"Like when?" I pushed the first doorbell on the sixth floor.

"In the park or in the car."

The door opened. "Chi e'?" said a guy about our age.

"Hi! We're from the Church of Jesus Christ. Is your father home?" I asked.

Before I even finished my question, the father was at the door, but he wasn't interested in our message. At least he was nice about it, though. He closed the door and Deiana pushed the next doorbell. "So what kind of car did you have?" I asked him.

"A Fiat 500," he said, looking indignant when I snickered. The "cinquecento" was probably the smallest car made by Fiat, so tiny it made a Volkswagon bug look big. "Better than a moped!" he added defensively.

"I'm sure! So, just how serious do you like to get in the park or in your 500?"

We heard some rustling in the apartment in front of us, so we knew someone was looking at us through the peep hole. Deiana decided to give his approach to the door, but he got no response. We went down to the next floor. I pushed the first doorbell.

"Well, if I know her well enough, we'd probably French kiss."

"Yeah?" I paused. "I hate to sound ignorant, but I've never kissed a girl before. Just exactly how do you go about French kissing?"

Deiana looked incredulous for a moment, but he knew me pretty well after two months, though I was sure he didn't know *why* I had never kissed a girl, and I would have preferred to die rather than ever tell him. "Well, when you kiss," he said, "you just put your tongue in her mouth and tickle the roof of her mouth. Girls love it."

"And what does she do?"

"Chi e′?" said an old, female voice from the back of the apartment.

"Good evening!" I said loudly. "We're two—"

"Chi e′?" the old woman shouted, a little closer to the door. It was useless to answer yet. "Chi e′?" she shouted again. Now she was almost close enough. "Chi e′?" she repeated yet another time, right at the door. I explained who we were and our purpose, but she was sure we were thieves and told us to go away. I pushed the next doorbell.

"Oh, girls do the same thing," Deiana continued. "Guys love it, too."

"I'll have to try it one day."

"You don't know what you're missing."

In the next building, we discussed relatives. Deiana almost died when he heard the country names of my Southern relatives, my Uncle Buford and Aunt Betty Jo, and my cousins Mary Lou, Thelma Rose, and Bertha Sue. A woman opened her door as Deiana was laughing, but fortunately, she was good-natured and liked to see two boys who seemed pretty decent. Since her husband was home, she let us in and we taught them our first lesson, about Joseph Smith, the Book of Mormon, and the restoration of the Church of Jesus Christ. They weren't terribly interested, but we left a Book of Mormon and a couple of pamphlets along with our card, which had the address of the local congregation and the missionaries' phone number. Who knows? At least we planted a seed.

Of all the different things we did as missionaries, tracting was one of my favorites because my companion and I were able to contact a lot of people and still have time to get to know each other better. We could discuss the work and new ideas, experiment with different door approaches, and get to meet with people in their homes where they felt most comfortable. It had taken me a while before I learned to enjoy it, of course, but it had almost always been better than referral taking was for me.

Not that tracting was always fun. After all, there was the time that woman had chased us out of her building with a pair of scissors, and over near Piazza Sempione last month when that man had pulled a gun on us, and there were a couple of doors shut in our faces each night along with being kicked out by portieri. But even those experiences were okay when shared with a friend.

I had always been afraid of having to be with a companion for twenty-four hours a day, every day. Surely there would be habits and characteristics that wouldn't blend well. That was true, I'd found out, but after a year and a half, I had learned to tolerate an awful lot of habits. I'd had a couple of rough companionships, but Deiana was not only okay, he was absolutely the best companion I'd had out of twelve so far. We had a lot of good times, but still there were days when having a good friend by my side constantly was the only way I survived emotionally or spiritually.

We had always been told, "Love the country, love the people, love your companion. Then you'll be an effective missionary." I'd always tried to put that into effect, and I'd found that it was true. All of that came together in my present companion, which made me appreciate him more than my other companions. But no one had prepared me to be separated from the people I had learned to love.

Love was a weird feeling for me, one I hadn't felt often, and it scared me a little. Once, when I was a child, my Sunday school teacher had asked us all to go home and tell our fathers that we loved them, saying that our fathers needed to hear that once in a while. That night right before I went to bed, when my father was in the kitchen getting something to drink, I'd said, "I love you, Daddy." He hadn't even looked at me. I supposed he'd felt awkward, but at the time I thought it meant he didn't love me at all.

I grew leery of the word "love" just after the one incident, and when my aunt told me she loved me a few years later, all I was able to manage in reply was, "I sure appreciate you, too." And whenever I felt particularly close to any other friend or relative, which hadn't been all that often, the only thing I'd been able to say was, "I like you." The word "love" just wouldn't come out of me. I felt it for Deiana, but I wasn't sure I'd actually be able to risk saying it again. I had tried a couple of times during the past few weeks, but the words simply would not come.

Now Deiana and I were probably going to be split up. I only had six more months before I went back to America. Why, I might not ever see Deiana again after two more days. Ever! I slipped my left arm around Deiana's right arm as we turned onto Via Livorno. It was common custom among Italian friends, even guys, to hold hands or walk arm in arm. I had quickly picked that up during my time with Deiana, although I knew I'd be clobbered if I ever tried that with an American companion.

The first time Deiana had held my hand was during a district meeting with the other elders and sisters all around us. I'd been so surprised I didn't know what to do. I could feel my face turning red, but I *liked* holding his hand, so I didn't pull away. Then one evening, I had casually been rubbing my neck to get a crick out of it, and Deiana had come over and given me a massage. To feel his strong hands against my skin was wonderful. *Wonderful.* I was so afraid I'd fall in love with him, and yet I never felt that any of the contact we had was sexual. It was the touching between two friends, and I thanked God he'd sent me to a country where I could actually touch another man, and it was *all right*.

It was time for a break, so Deiana and I walked over to a nearby bar and ordered two glasses of Ferrarelle orange soda, my favorite. We watched a teenaged kid playing a pinball machine for a few minutes, and we talked to the bartender for a moment. He said he'd had the missionary lessons a few years ago, but he didn't care to hear any more. "Keep on working, though. I believe what you're doing is good." He wouldn't let us pay for the sodas. Thanking the bartender, we left and headed back to Via Livorno.

Deiana suggested a pee break then, but there was no place nearby with a public bathroom other than the bar we'd just left, which Deiana didn't want to return to. So he led me into the next apartment building and up to the top floor. Then he found a door which led up to the roof of the building. It was dark up here, but light enough to see because of the street lights and apartment buildings all around. Deiana walked to the edge of the roof and unzipped his pants. "Come on," he said, smiling.

I had a hard time peeing in the presence of another man, and even using a public restroom by myself was difficult because I was always afraid someone else was about to come in. But this was Deiana, and I felt more comfortable with him than I ever had with anyone else, so I walked up to the edge of the roof and unzipped, too.

"Let's go," he said, and started urinating, right over the edge of the roof. I couldn't believe it. But a thrill went through me as I contemplated being so naughty, and I soon followed his example. When we finished, he laughed, and we headed back for the door leading down to the stairwell again.

The rest of the evening went fairly well. We only got in one more door, and that for only fifteen minutes, but we did have some good talks with people in the hall. One man said he'd come to church on Sunday, but of the hundreds who had said that to me, I had yet to see someone actually come out to church. There was always the chance, though. We'd see.

Deiana and I also got to talk some more to each other in between doors and buildings. I thought I knew almost everything about him already, but I did learn a couple of new things. For example, he could say some English curse words quite well. That jerk on the moped who spit at us didn't know what was going on, but I sure did. He had that pronunciation and accent just right. I wondered who'd taught him.

We left our zone and started back to the apartment at about 9:00. We only had to wait a few minutes on Nomentana before a 136 came along. There weren't many people on the bus, so Deiana grinned at me and said in English, "Bus Surfing, U.S.A."

"In bocc'al lupo, Anziano," I said. It was an expression used to wish one luck, which translated literally to "in the mouth of the wolf." Legend had it that Rome had been founded by Romulus and Remus, two orphans who had been raised by a wolf, so the expression was a wish that the recipient would be as fortunate as Romulus and Remus had been. The phrase had sounded ominous to me the first time I heard it, but I'd seen that a lot of things which seemed negative at first could turn out to be positive in the end.

Elder Deiana and I started bus surfing then. We balanced ourselves in the back of the bus and tried to stand without holding onto or leaning on anything. I cheated on a couple of curves and almost fell at one stop, but Deiana had been practicing longer and was really rather good. My balance had been getting a little better lately, though, since I'd been practicing more with Deiana. A few odd stares did come our way, especially from one old, large woman in black who scowled at us several times, but we were so used to being stared at as missionaries that it didn't bother us at all. We either ignored the staring people or smiled back at them.

Within twenty minutes, we were back on Franco Sacchetti, so we pushed the button and hopped off the bus. At least at night we could get off at the same stop. Last week, when we had been coming home for lunch at 1:30, the bus had been so crowded that only Deiana could squeeze off at the right stop. Then I'd had to battle for a minute with a "pasta mamma" and some young teens and get off at the next stop a couple of blocks away.

As we were slowly walking back to the apartment, Deiana looped his right arm around my left, and he rested his head on my shoulder. We looked up at our building and saw that the lights were on in our apartment. The other elders were already home. We rode the elevator up to the third floor and started to walk down the hall toward our apartment.

Deiana didn't slow down as he spoke. "Ti voglio bene. Sai?"

I didn't hesitate, either, in my reply. "I love you, too, Elder."

The Hotel Room

"I can't tell what's more fun," said Sefton, "sex with you or listening to your stories."

I wasn't sure exactly how to take that, my income and a great deal of my ego resting on the assumption that I was reasonably hot. In the end, I decided he simply meant I was good at both tasks. And it meant he'd enjoyed a story about someone learning to accept his orientation. I hoped I'd planted a seed. Sefton was sitting up in bed with his legs crossed, his head turned toward me, his face eager.

"I see you served a mission to Italy," he said.

"I won't tell you if that's a true story or not," I protested.

"I can tell what's true and what isn't true. I have the gift of the Holy Ghost, remember."

I didn't say anything.

"You still fluent?"

"I read books in Italian for fun, and I can say a few sentences in a couple of other languages. And what are you good at besides your sexual prowess?" I asked with a teasing smile. A door shut loudly one room over, making us both jump, and breaking the playful mood.

"Speaking on the floor in support of legislation," he answered with a straight face. "Or speaking on the floor in opposition to legislation."

If only I could encourage him to do the latter tomorrow. I hoped that all these stories would indoctrinate him a bit more into gay culture, help him identify more with gays. But there were still women who voted against reproductive freedom, working class people who voted against raising taxes on the wealthy. It wasn't only closeted gays who voted against their own best interest.

In a way, it sounded lofty to vote for a higher ideal, even if it affected you personally in a negative way. But these "higher ideals" usually affected 99% of the population in a negative way and only consistently benefitted the elite. I wasn't sure that was so lofty. Even when these laws did indeed negatively impact only a small minority, I still wasn't convinced that "a little" oppression was ever justified.

God, I'd have hated being a politician.

"Surely, there are other things you do well, too," I pressed.

Sefton shrugged. "I run," he said. "I've only made it up to a half marathon so far, but one day I'd like to go the whole distance."

"Well, that's pretty impressive," I said. I reached over and rubbed his calf.

Sefton smiled nervously in embarrassment.

"You don't like being complimented, do you?" I asked.

He frowned. "I always feel like a big sham. People think I'm good. But they wouldn't think so if they *knew*."

"People think highly of Barney Frank. He was elected lots of times."

Sefton sneered. "It only matters if the *right* people admire you."

"Like the electorate?"

"The electorate of Idaho isn't like that in New England."

"So move. You've heard of real estate agents, haven't you?"

Sefton stared at me as if I'd suggested he sell one of his kidneys. I was afraid the discussion was growing too serious, and I had already surmised that Sefton wasn't the type to handle that well.

"You know," I said, "I have another story which addresses this pretty effectively."

"Then why would I want to hear it?" he asked grumpily.

I laughed. "Oh, Sefton, you have such a good sense of humor. But you need to learn how to discuss things more directly." He looked at me in consternation, and before he could protest any further, I began.

Sex Organs

"Oh, my god."

"Larry, we'll do everything we can to fight."

"This can't be real."

"Don't give up. We'll overcome this. It's not the end of the world."

Larry smiled. It *was* the end of the world. He hadn't been so happy in all his life, in all his seventy years. Pancreatic cancer. He wanted to get down on his knees right there in Dr. Kramer's office and praise God for His goodness.

"Is there any treatment that will cure this, or will it just prolong my suffering?"

"There's always hope."

Larry smiled again. There clearly was no way to survive. Tears came to his eyes. Ten years ago when he'd had his heart attack, he'd submitted to placing a stent in his heart, and he'd suffered some unappetizing changes in diet. He'd *wanted* to die of a heart attack, but not fighting to survive would have been suicide, and that was as terrible a sin as homosexuality. If he'd managed to stay a virgin his entire life, he wasn't going to ruin his chances for the afterlife by losing points at the very end.

But terminal cancer to a vital organ. There was nothing he could do about that. His test was finally over. His trial. His torture.

"Please don't cry, Larry."

"How long do I have?"

"You know we can't say."

"How long?"

Dr. Kramer shrugged. "Six months."

Larry nodded. "Thanks, Doc."

Larry drove home slowly. The trees looked greener, the flowers redder and yellower, the sky bluer.

Back in his house, Larry got on the internet and booked a flight for Atlanta. His favorite destinations were San Francisco, New York, and Toronto, but he thought he'd start out with a tamer city. The Pole Vault in Atlanta was a reliable first way to celebrate. Larry made a reservation at the Marriott. He liked Marriott because he was a Mormon, too. And Marriott had shown himself to be sensitive to gay issues, though of course he couldn't be too supportive or he'd risk excommunication.

Larry had longed for sex almost sixty years, but his longing for the Celestial Kingdom was even stronger. He'd prayed at first to be made heterosexual. When that didn't work, he'd prayed for paralysis or coma. Those hadn't happened, either. Finally, he'd begun praying for death, but after thirty years of unanswered prayers, the doctor's diagnosis was like seeing a vision of Jesus Christ. It was a miracle.

"Cole, this is Larry from Salt Lake. How are you?"

"Hi, Larry. You coming to Atlanta?"

"I want to arrange another 'date.' On the 17th. Around 6:00, so you still have time to dance at the club later."

"Sounds great. I'd love to see you again."

"And can you find someone else to come along? You know my type, and what I like."

"There's a new guy, Cliff. He'll be perfect. Want me to send you a picture?"

Larry considered. He loved looking at naked men, but he'd worked hard over the years to avoid addiction to pornography. There was no sense risking it now. "No, surprise me."

Larry gave Cole the address of the Marriott and his cell number, and he started packing. Normally, he planned trips weeks, even months, in advance. He already had one set up for San Francisco five weeks from now. But this diagnosis called for immediate celebration. He was willing to pay extra for a last-minute ticket.

After he packed for his flight the following morning, Larry sat on his bed, wondering what to do. He had no friends he could call. He'd stopped attending Single Adult activities decades ago. It was too painful to see everyone else pairing up. He never accepted callings at church because it meant involvement with people who talked incessantly about their happy families. Larry went to Sacrament meeting, Sunday school, and Priesthood. He didn't volunteer answers. He didn't ask questions. It was too agonizing to have human contact that was never quite enough.

Larry remembered the interviews with the bishop when he was in his twenties. Why aren't you married? When are you going to settle down and raise a family? It started getting serious, the bishop almost threatening him if he didn't do his duty as a man. Finally, Larry had to "admit" to having sustained an injury while serving in the army. It was during peacetime, so he described it as a "training accident," but thankfully, the bishop left him alone after that.

The problem with this story was that it meant Larry could never confess his sin of masturbation to the bishop. He could therefore never fully repent and be forgiven, and that might affect his salvation. Of course, true repentance meant giving up the sin, and Larry had never been able to do that, either. He figured it was a compromise. "I won't have sex with another man. I won't ruin a woman's life. But in exchange, You'll have to grant me the right to touch myself."

He knew it was still a sin, but he watched TV. He watched movies. He knew perfectly well that there wasn't a man in a million who had *never* had sex. He wasn't sure he qualified for the lower part of the Celestial Kingdom, the part set aside for ministering angels who would never be gods, but he hoped at least for the Terrestrial, where "good, decent people" were to go. In his heart of hearts, though, he still hoped for a bell curve. For a gay man, he'd done exceptionally well. He deserved amnesty and admittance to the top kingdom. He wanted it. He had earned it.

Larry looked at the phone again, wanting to talk to someone. He'd never had a roommate, of course, or a best friend. It would have been too difficult not to confide, not to want a comforting shoulder.

He smiled. Soon he'd see his mother again. He could talk to someone then.

Larry lay back on the bed and rubbed his crotch through his pants. He smiled as he felt a hardening under the thick cloth. He started fantasizing about what would take place in Atlanta. Larry always hired two escorts at a time. He had them act out various scenarios. Perhaps one of them would play a Roman slave dealer who had to show Larry a prospective slave to purchase. The slave dealer would slowly unrobe the slave to let Larry see the entire piece of merchandise. He'd get the slave hard to show how well he'd be able to service his new master. The dealer would kiss the man to gauge how passionate he could be.

But Larry would never let the two escorts actually have sex. It was a sin to commit homosexual acts, and Larry couldn't allow causing others to sin to be on his conscience. He just needed to see beautiful men, sexy men, impassioned men.

But no sex.

Larry unzipped his pants and pulled out his penis. He stroked it lovingly and closed his eyes.

No, he was not going to do this. He was going to be strong.

Yet he needed *something*. Larry walked to the kitchen and ate a peach. Then he ate a banana. Somehow, he still wasn't satisfied.

He paced back and forth across the living room for twenty minutes. He looked at his prints of the famous Arnold Friberg paintings on his walls. The stripling warriors, Samuel the Lamanite, Moroni burying the gold plates. He rubbed his crotch again.

Larry sat at the kitchen table and thought. He'd never hired an escort in Salt Lake before. It always seemed too risky. But he needed to see another human being. Maybe touch his arm or his chest. He always picked up the gay paper and knew there were ads.

He nodded. He was going to do it.

Around 3:30, Jeffrey knocked on his door. Larry smiled when he opened it. "You're perfect," said Larry.

Jeffrey smiled and came inside. "Nice house. You have money."

"Not really. I just don't have kids."

"What do you want to do?"

"I want to see you look hot and bothered. I want to watch you slowly, very slowly take off your clothes and rub yourself all over. I want you to look like you've just got to get off, but I don't want you to actually do it."

Larry didn't know why he couldn't allow himself to ask an escort to masturbate for him. If it was a small enough sin that he could do it himself, then what would be the harm in ordering someone else to beat off? Larry didn't really know; he just understood it would be a sin, and he didn't do it.

"Right here?"

"This way."

The two men walked into Larry's bedroom, and Larry sat on the edge of his bed and licked his lips. Jeffrey walked slowly about, pulling at his collar a little, wiping his brow, and finally ripping off his shirt. He caressed his stomach and his nipples, traced a line up and down his chest, and let the line go down to his crotch.

He rubbed his crotch lightly for a moment, sighed, and then squeezed. He moaned and slowly unbuttoned his jeans. With each button he undid, Jeffrey would moan and squeeze again. Finally, the pants fell down around Jeffrey's ankles, and Larry watched in delight as the escort's huge penis throbbed against his underwear. There was a little drop of pre-cum on the fabric. Larry rubbed his own crotch for a second, too, but quickly stopped. He was not going to masturbate while with another man. That would be sex, not masturbation.

"I need you," said Jeffrey.

Larry smiled and nodded for him to go on.

"I really need you." Jeffrey moved up to the bed and put his hand on Larry's chest.

"No. No touching."

Jeffrey removed his hand but still stood right next to Larry, his bulging underwear only a centimeter away from Larry's leg. Larry closed his eyes. The pain was almost unbearable. But he smiled. Soon he'd feel the pain of his cancer, and then everything would be fine.

When he opened his eyes, Larry saw Jeffrey's face only inches from his own. He could feel the warmth across the brief space between them. He tried to move backward, but Jeffrey moved forward. "Just a little kiss," he whispered. "I don't usually kiss my clients, but I want to kiss you. You're different. You're special."

Larry's first instinct was to say no. He'd never kissed a man before, and while kissing didn't sound like a serious sin in itself, he was scared to cross the line into physical contact.

But he was about to die. What if there was no kissing for celibate angels in heaven? Maybe this was his only chance in all of eternity for a kiss.

"Yes," he breathed.

Jeffrey leaned in closer, and his lips met Larry's. It was the most glorious thing Larry had ever experienced in his life. Something that wonderful couldn't be a sin.

Jeffrey pushed Larry gently onto his back and climbed on top of him. Larry protested weakly, but he was fully clothed, wasn't he? It wasn't as if he were guilty of petting. Then he felt Jeffrey's hand on his crotch, and he moaned in protest. Jeffrey seemed to think that this was a good moan and squeezed harder. Now he forced his tongue into Larry's mouth. Larry tried to pull away, but Jeffrey seemed so heavy.

And yet that weight seemed altogether heavenly. Larry couldn't bring himself to push Jeffrey away.

Jeffrey started unbuttoning Larry's shirt. He moaned in protest another time. Then again, it wasn't as if a man's chest was a sex organ. There was no real sin to let Jeffrey touch it. He reached up to feel Jeffrey's chest as well.

Jeffrey got out of the bed and pulled his underwear off. Now he was completely naked in front of Larry. Larry could see something glisten on the end of his penis and stared. Jeffrey touched the tip of his penis and then brought his finger to Larry's lips. Larry kept them pressed firmly shut, but he couldn't resist the curiosity. In seventy years, he'd never tasted semen or even pre-cum. It was a sin to find out, but he licked his lips and felt a warmth spread through his chest.

It tasted good.

Jeffrey reached over and started unbuckling Larry's belt.

"No. I have to draw the line. We can't do any more."

"I just want to look at you. That's fair, isn't it?"

Larry considered. Just looking wasn't a sin. Or much of one, anyway. He took off all his clothes and lay on the bed. Jeffrey climbed back on the bed, prying Larry's legs apart. "No sex. Just looking," said Larry.

Jeffrey smiled. "A touch won't hurt." He put his hand gently on Larry's penis.

"No. Don't touch my penis. It's a sex organ. I'll go to hell."

Jeffrey giggled. "Okay, okay." He took his hand off and knelt, looking at Larry. Then he smiled again and wet his finger. He reached under Larry's balls and found his asshole. "Your ass isn't a sex organ, is it?"

Larry frowned.

"Is it?" Jeffrey repeated.

"It is if you put your penis in it."

"Then I won't put my penis in it." He pushed his finger forward, and Larry felt it bearing past his sphincter.

"No."

"A finger isn't a sex organ."

Larry frowned again. That was true enough, too, wasn't it?

Jeffrey pushed his finger in deeper, pulled it almost all the way out, and pushed it in again. Larry had never felt anything so wonderful in his life. He relaxed and enjoyed it for a moment, but then he understood that despite the rationalizing, it was still a sin. He was almost finished his test. He couldn't allow himself to fail now.

"Okay, thanks," said Larry. "That's enough."

"I want to make you come."

"Oh, god, no."

"I can do it without ever touching your penis, I swear."

This thought intrigued Larry, and he considered again, but then he shook his head.

Jeffrey's eyebrows furrowed. "Old man, you are a real pain in the ass." He lifted Larry's legs in one quick motion and in seconds had thrust his penis deep inside Larry. Larry yelled from the sudden pain, but then Jeffrey clamped his mouth on top of his. He began pumping away, pumping away, and Larry could feel that enormous penis sliding back and forth against his sphincter. After a few moments, it stopped hurting and began to feel good. He tried to push Jeffrey away, but Jeffrey was too young and strong.

Then something horrible happened. Just as Larry heard Jeffrey's panting reach a crescendo that told him the youth was getting close to climax, Larry felt his own penis burning. With one last, deep thrust, Jeffrey came, groaning heavily, and a second later, Larry came as well.

But he'd been raped. It wasn't as if he'd done anything voluntarily. He was still innocent.

Jeffrey pulled out and got dressed while Larry lay there stunned. "That'll be $200, old man." He held out his hand.

Larry continued to lie there.

"Come on, geezer. Pay up."

Larry sat up, his semen dripping off his stomach, and went to gather his wallet. He pulled out some twenties, and Jeffrey stuffed them in his pocket and left. Larry sat back on the edge of his bed.

He'd liked it. He could confess and repent, though, and hold out without repeating the incident another six months. Six months wasn't forever. He could do it.

But he'd crossed the line. Could he see Cole in Atlanta and not touch him? What would it be like to have a man come in his mouth? What would it be like to enter another man?

What would it be like to love someone?

No. He was going to be pure when he died. His parents and grandparents had all lived well into their nineties. God was merciful to let him die at age seventy. Larry would show his appreciation and be a good boy. The brain was the biggest sex organ, and he was going to keep it in control.

The phone rang. Larry looked at his watch. It was just 5:00. He sighed and picked up the receiver. "Hello?"

"Larry?" said a breathless voice. "It's Dr. Kramer. I had to call you right away." He paused just a moment. "There's been a terrible mistake. Your lab results got mixed up with someone else's. You don't have cancer. Do you hear me? You're perfectly fine. Healthy as a horse. I wanted to let you know as soon as I found out. I didn't want you to suffer needlessly."

Larry sat holding the phone in silence.

"Larry? Larry? You okay?"

"That's wonderful news," said Larry dully. "Thanks for calling." He hung up the phone in a daze. He sat there motionless for fifteen minutes, and then for another twenty. Finally, he blinked and looked about the room.

He needed to talk to someone.

But who? Larry didn't even have an address book.

Larry sat staring at the floor for another quarter of an hour. He needed human contact. What was he to do?

His eyes fell upon the gay newspaper again. He picked it up listlessly and turned to the back. Sighing, he picked up the phone and dialed. "Dallas, can you come to my place in an hour?" He listened a moment and then continued. "Yes, I have the money here." He nodded silently. "See you soon."

Larry sat naked on his bed for a few minutes longer. Then he licked some flakes of his dried cum mindlessly, while a single tear caught on his cheek.

The Hotel Room

"How do I compare sexually to other men?" asked Sefton when I'd finished.

I was astounded. *That's* what he was thinking about as I told this story? Sheesh. Such a typical man. Sometimes I wished I were a lesbian.

"You're actually pretty good," I said honestly, trying to keep the irritation out of my voice. I felt he had just ignored me for the past fifteen minutes, and my feelings were hurt.

"Really?"

He sounded so genuinely happy at my response that some of my irritation dissipated, but only slightly. "Yes. I suppose you realize I've had sex with a lot of guys. Even before I became an escort. Most are okay, but nothing so wonderful you feel you need to repeat the experience. Some are downright disasters. And then there are the special few you'd like to see again."

"Like me?" he asked hopefully.

"I'd like you to call me again sometime."

"Will you charge me?"

Every once in a while, a customer thought he was so extraordinary that I would want to have sex with him free of charge. And to be honest, it was true a few times. But I made it a hard and fast rule that I only dated "regular" guys. A client always remained a client. No dating there.

Still, with several more hours yet to fill up, it wouldn't hurt to string Sefton along a bit more. Anything to keep him from making that vote.

"Sefton, I'm going to tell you my real name." This would make him feel he was making progress, even if I wasn't directly answering his question. "It's not Matt. It's Houston."

"Houston? *That* sounds like a stage name."

"Maybe it does. It's also uncommon. There are lots of Matts but not many Houstons. I don't want to make it too easy for clients to find me if things don't go well."

Sefton's eyes grew kind. "Do you have many jerks?" he asked softly.

I shrugged. "Once in a while. They're in every profession. Don't *you* have to deal with jerks sometimes?"

His gaze hardened, and I regretted the comment. No need to turn his thoughts to the Senate floor again. "Perhaps you could come to my place next time," I suggested, hoping to steer the conversation back. "I don't imagine you'd want to go to a restaurant or anything like that."

"No." He shook his head. "No restaurant. And I'm not sure about coming to your place just yet. Maybe we could meet here again next weekend?"

"I'd love to, Sefton. Perhaps we could watch a movie or talk about what we want most in the world, or do whatever you like. And of course have sex." How he voted tomorrow would decide if I charged again, and how much. And maybe whether or not I even went public. Sefton was being agreeable enough so far, but I'd certainly seen politicians say the right thing to voters before an election and then do the wrong thing once in office. I wondered if Sefton were playing me the way I was playing him.

"A couple of times." He grabbed my crotch and squeezed gently.

"At least."

He smiled like a boy who'd just won his first race, and I picked up his hand and set it on my chest. "I know it's getting late, but are you game for one more story?"

"You're incorrigible," he said, groaning. "But go ahead. You're pretty good at this."

"I believe we should strive for excellence in all things." I wagged my finger like an annoying teacher. "Some things, like sex, or like storytelling, take a lot of practice."

"I might want to practice sex one more time tonight after you practice telling one more story."

I gave him my best Mona Lisa smile and began to speak.

Partying with St. Roch

I could see that Dennis had a drinking problem. It wasn't as bad as Glenn's had been, of course. I'd dated Glenn for almost a year before he died of cirrhosis, holed up in his apartment with empty beer cans around his bed. He'd frequently point to my flat stomach after we had sex and say, "You may have a six-pack, but *I've* got a whole keg," and then he would pat his extended abdomen. I'd thought it was just a beer belly, but some of that enlargement was due to his damaged liver. After that experience, I vowed I'd never date another drinker.

Then I met Dennis at the Unitarian church in Uptown New Orleans on Nashville. We were both excommunicated Mormons, and we hit it off singing about a God who loved all people equally. We dated for five months and then moved in together, about one month before Dennis's T-cells dropped to 50 and he was diagnosed with full-blown AIDS.

It was late 1989, and we were looking forward to New Year's, hoping for a repeat of the Gay Nineties, at least in name, working together for gay rights with several organizations, not the least of which was ACT UP, carrying signs and shouting slogans in front of City Hall as we demanded more access to medicines. Shortly after we moved in together on St. Roch, just off of Chartres in the Marigny, Dennis developed an addiction to Coke.

That's Coke with a capital C.

He began having me purchase every three-liter bottle of the off brand the local Schwegmann's grocery stocked when I went to do our weekly shopping. I'd pile twelve of the monstrous bottles into my cart and plod my way to the checkout. Every single week, people would smile and say, "You having a party?"

"Nothing but fun at my house," I'd reply, smiling back.

"Kirk, you only bought eight bottles today," Dennis complained to me this afternoon. "I'll never make it through the week."

"I'll stop at the store again tomorrow."

"I need this. I get so little pleasure out of life."

"I'll stop at the store again tomorrow."

The sodas were not diet. I was afraid that at any moment, Dennis would have diabetes to add to his problems, but something about the HIV or his particular metabolism seemed to defy the sugar overload. He remained thin as a rail despite a full daily allotment of calories just from the cola alone. His other favorite treat was chocolate, which was a debatable violation of the Word of Wisdom. And perhaps because the caffeine kept him from fully hydrating despite the vast amounts of liquid he consumed, he also drank a great deal of black tea.

"Do you think I'm a hedonist, Kirk?" Dennis asked. "Do you think I should be obeying all the commandments now that I'm about to die?"

"Shut up and fuck me," I said, forcing a smile.

I was still negative, and Dennis always used a condom when we had sex. The irony was that he was basically a top. He'd only bottomed maybe three or four times ever, but he'd done it just once without a condom, and now he was paying the price. Every day, priests and pastors across the country were still proclaiming that AIDS was God's punishment for our abominable sins, thereby infecting everyone with their hatred. It was impossible not to wonder if they were right. Every evening as I kissed the man I loved goodnight, I would look into his face and wonder if God really despised us this much. One of the last things I heard my stake president say after he told me I was excommunicated was, "If Heavenly Father still loves you, He'll give you AIDS to help you repent. It's so much kinder than letting you live in your sins for a lifetime, thinking you're not sinning. I'll pray that God gives you AIDS, for your own good." He smiled and held out his hand warmly, as if he'd just said something comforting.

My hand stayed by my side, and his finally dropped as well, a look of confusion on his face. I turned and walked out of his office, and I never went to an LDS church again. Mormonism had always been my rock before, "the one and only true church." Four years passed, in fact, before I ever entered any other church at all. A friend invited me to a meeting at the MCC in the Bywater, in an ancient red brick building along the levee. I didn't like the congregation, so a few months later, I tried a Dignity meeting with some gay Catholics. I didn't care for that, either. I attended a Reform synagogue Uptown on St. Charles and liked that well enough, but I was afraid to stop praying "in the name of Jesus Christ," even though I wasn't sure I even believed in Jesus Christ anymore. I realized I was being superstitious, not religious. I attended a Methodist meeting on North Rampart in the Quarter and then an Episcopalian service Uptown and a Hare Krishna meeting on Esplanade. At last I stumbled upon the Unitarian meeting. I had been just about to give up my quest as pointless when I listened to a blonde woman with dreadlocks give a sermon on the importance of protecting the environment, and I decided to come back a second time. I'd been attending ever since.

"Really?" said Dennis, looking doubtful, almost mournful. "You're still attracted to me?"

"I want you, mister."

I grabbed my crotch, and Dennis's eyes lit up. He hurried over to the dresser and pulled out the two nametags I'd had made. He slipped one on his shirt pocket that said, "Elder Top—The Church of Jesus Christ of Latter-gay Saints" and handed mine for me to put on my pocket, "Elder Bottom" and with the same fake Church name. Dennis leaned forward to kiss me, rubbing against me and smiling as our two missionary nametags clicked against each other. Then, despite the costume, he took off his shirt and knelt in front of me, unzipping my pants as I rubbed his head, trying not to be distracted by the large black Kaposi's lesions on his shoulders and back. He didn't fuck me as I'd suggested but just sucked me off. I watched as his head moved back and forth, wanting to memorize every sexual encounter with him, so that I could replay them after he was gone. With a final thrust, I came, and then Dennis smiled and stood up.

"Your turn?" I asked, pointing to his zipper.

He shook his head. "All I want is more Coke. I know it's a pain, but can you go to another store?"

I nodded and went to grab my cart again. We didn't have a car, and the Schwegmann's on Claiborne was the only store truly within walking distance, about nine blocks from the apartment. The next closest was a grocery on Franklin. I walked the five blocks to the bus stop, waited for almost twenty minutes, and then boarded the 57. A few minutes later, I was at the store.

There were no three-liter bottles here of the off brand that Dennis preferred, but there were several two-liter bottles of regular Coke. I'd tried making this substitution for Dennis before with negative results. He wanted what he wanted, and nothing else would do. It could be annoying, but how could I deny him what few indulgences he had left in life?

If what the Church taught were true, there'd be no Coke in heaven. I'd never even dared try a sip until I went to my first gay bar.

I wondered if it were true that the Church owned lots of stock in Coca-Cola.

I pushed my cart along the pavement until I arrived at the bus stop. What could I try next? There was a Rouse's up closer to the lake. Since I was already taking the bus, I supposed it didn't matter how many blocks I had to go once I was sitting down. The bus jerked to a halt in front of me fifteen minutes later, and I dragged my cart on board. I was the only white person in the vehicle. Whites in general were afraid to ride the buses in New Orleans, afraid they'd be murdered by all those "low-class" blacks who filled the seats. While I did get a few cold stares once in a while, obviously most other passengers ignored me completely. Once, I'd run into my Sunday school teacher Theautrey on the Elysian Fields bus and said hi and shaken his hand. At the Unitarian church the next Sunday, he admitted he'd felt two conflicting emotions: one, surprise that a white person would acknowledge him in public, and two, embarrassment in front of other blacks that *he* was friends with a white person himself.

As a Mormon, I'd learned about how blacks had been cursed with a dark skin for their lack of dedication to God in the Pre-existence. While I'd grown up watching *Diff'rent Strokes* and *The Jeffersons* and didn't feel I harbored much prejudice, whenever I saw a news report of another black murderer or listened to the uneducated speech of blacks around me, I'd doubt just a little my belief that all people were equal. Maybe it wasn't oppression and lack of opportunity that hurt this community. What if they really were inferior spirits? Even while listening to Theautrey teach a class on Sundays and feeling impressed with his knowledge, I'd doubt. Maybe he had some white blood, I'd think. Maybe that was why he was so smart.

I'd hate myself for thinking these things and then get mad at the Mormons all over again for filling my head with such nonsense. Gays weren't bad. Blacks weren't inferior. What kind of religion went around spreading such a plague of hateful teachings in the first place?

Then I'd wonder again if I was going to hell.

I climbed out of the bus across the street from Rouse's and headed for the store. I went straight for the soda aisle, ready to be finished with this interminable chore and get back home to relax. I worked all week at the public library under a tyrannical manager and then came home to a sick partner. Saturday was my day to have fun, and I had to take my fun when I could get it. I tried to make these outings an escape from the confines of my apartment, but all I really wanted to do was listen to Roxette while putting together a thousand-piece jigsaw puzzle of Notre Dame or the Taj Mahal.

No three-liter bottles.

Why did Dennis have to drink so much? Was it his way of thumbing his nose at God?

I looked over the soda section a second time to make sure I wasn't missing anything. There was a section for three-liter bottles, all right, but there weren't any stocked. Was there an epidemic of cola addiction out there?

"Excuse me," I said, stopping a young black man with a nametag. "Could you check in back to see if you have any more of the three-liter bottles?"

The man looked at me, looked at the empty shelf, looked at me again with his lip curled ever so slightly, and headed off without a word. I waited fifteen minutes and then decided to try one last store, a new one that had opened next to the projects near Canal. This would be the last stop on my pilgrimage, regardless of the outcome.

I arrived thirty-five minutes later and pushed my cart quickly to the soda aisle. There was a lone three-liter bottle. An elderly woman looked as if she was contemplating it. I debated whether or not to snatch the bottle before she had a chance to reach for it, but I bit my lip and waited till she slowly moved on down the aisle. I put the bottle in my cart, added one more item from a few aisles away, and headed for the checkout.

Dennis was not going to be pleased.

Was I a bad partner for giving up before I'd accomplished what Dennis asked of me? The man was dying, after all. He'd be gone in only a few months. Couldn't I sacrifice just a little more for him? Perhaps this proved that fleeting gay relationships were a poor substitute for "true" eternal marriage. It was what I felt every Sunday, too, that my new religion was only a lackluster replacement for the real thing, no matter how much I told myself I preferred these services to the Sacrament and Priesthood meetings of before.

Could one be inoculated against the infection of self-doubt?

I dragged my cart off the steps of the bus twenty minutes later and pushed the metal cage ahead of me slowly, careful going over the cracked and uneven sidewalks of the Marigny. I passed the funeral home and the home of a gay hairdresser who was Clyde Barrow's cousin and then passed the home of a cute guy who routinely invited me to come in whenever he saw me walk by. I always politely refused, of course. He wasn't out today. I walked past the Lion's Inn gay bed and breakfast and finally made it to St. Roch.

The patron saint of the plague.

I unlocked the door underneath the balcony and headed up the stairs. "Kirk! I was afraid something had happened to you!"

"I could only find one more bottle."

Dennis stared at the bottle in disappointment and then managed a smile. "Maybe there will be more later in the week. I just want you to spend the rest of the day with me. We have so little time left together. Tell me more of your mission stories from Germany. You know I like that."

Dennis sat down on the sofa eagerly, and I poured him a glass of cola. Then I opened my other purchase, my first bottle of red wine, and poured myself a drink, too. I brought both glasses over to the coffee table and set them down. Dennis picked up his and looked at mine for a long moment without saying anything. Then I picked up mine and took a sip. Not bad.

"Tell me again about that time you decked your zone leader," said Dennis, leaning back and smiling.

"Well, naturally, it was an accident," I began. I sat back on the sofa, too, and Dennis swung his legs up so that his feet were resting in my lap. I sipped my wine with one hand and rubbed his feet with the other. I looked over at the man I loved, and wondered how I was going to fit the whole of eternity into the next few months. "It all started the day my zone leader told me in front of everyone that I didn't measure up to his expectations…"

I continued with my story, distracted by a new lesion on Dennis's leg. I began embellishing, just to add some variety, and Dennis grinned as I went on.

These are the good old days, I realized as I talked. One day soon, I'd look back and miss these times. I tried to memorize every detail of the room, the torn vinyl sofa we'd bought at Goodwill and had a friend deliver, the coffee table I'd carried two blocks from a garage sale, a mediocre piece of art Dennis had painted. When I finished my story, Dennis asked for another, this one about the middle-aged German man who'd fucked me one day when I'd broken the mission rules and took a long walk on my own.

We both smiled as I began telling the story. When I finished, I poured Dennis another glass of cola, and I sipped more of my wine. Then I had Dennis tell me one of his own favorite mission stories, back when he thought it was a healthy thing to spread the teachings of the Church. We smiled and laughed and drank, happy for a few brief moments on the torn sofa.

In the back of my mind, I wondered where I'd packed my Book of Mormon, and if maybe I should read for a while after Dennis fell asleep.

The Hotel Room

Sefton said nothing at first when I finished but climbed out of the bed and hugged himself as if he were cold. I thought he might put his robe on, which would be a bad sign, but he didn't. "I see that things don't always work out well for gays, either, do they?" he said and headed for the bathroom. He left the door open, and I could soon hear his stream hitting the water. He stopped at the dresser, took the paper covering off a glass, and returned to the bathroom, filling his glass at the sink.

When he walked back to the bed, the glass was still half full, and Sefton offered it to me. I noticed there was a drop of urine hanging off the end of his penis, and I leaned forward to lap it up before taking the offered glass.

"Gays are sick," Sefton muttered under his breath.

I laughed. "Most gays are just as boring as heterosexuals," I replied. "I promise you. It's just that once you're outside the normal rulebook, you get to decide for yourself what you're comfortable with. You enjoyed fucking earlier. Lots of people, even gays, are disgusted by anal sex." Sefton was still standing in front of me, apparently in no hurry to move away from my degenerate mouth.

"Well, it *is* disgusting," he said. "It's just that there are so few options with the available plumbing."

"Now you're talking like an independent man." I smoothed out the rumpled sheets and patted them.

"Independent," Sefton said softly, sitting down dejectedly. "I wonder if I could ever really switch parties. It wouldn't be a complete shift to the Dark Side. But I'd feel a little freer to make my own decisions."

"Making your own decisions is good," I agreed. I listened to myself, sounding so knowledgeable and confident. But I remembered that night when Derrick told me to run, and I did. I'd let him make the decision. Maybe I'd made a decision to *let* him make the decision, and it was something I'd regretted ever since.

I forced myself to focus on Sefton again, patting his leg.

"I don't know," he said.

"Sefton, tell me one thing you'd really like to do that you've never done before."

"You mean sexually?"

"It can be sexual if you want. But I really meant anything at all."

"Well, I'd like to skydive just once. And experience weightlessness in one of those planes that dive."

"And why don't you? There must be skydiving trips over in Idaho with all that land out there."

Sefton frowned. "It might look…frivolous."

"You can't spend your whole life worrying about what others might think. Besides, even President Bush went skydiving."

"That's true."

"So do it. And if you scream like a girl, no one will hear you. Just have fun."

"Fun," he said gloomily.

"Don't you believe in having fun at all?" I realized I was revisiting our earlier discussion.

"Man is, that he might have joy," he said. I remembered the quote.

"Well then."

He shook his head. "It's just that somehow it's different for me. For righteous gays in general, I suppose. We have to suffer to make up for our weakness."

I gritted my teeth at the term. "So suffer already. Fast an extra day. Give more money to charity. Study the statistics on a really tricky piece of legislation. But that doesn't mean you can't have a bowl of ice cream once in a while."

"Like I'm doing tonight with you."

I put my hands on his face and turned him to look at me. "Tonight, you're pouring salt all over the ice cream so it won't taste as good. Have some *real* ice cream."

Sefton's look grew pensive, and while that made me hopeful, I was also afraid he wasn't up to the task of honest self-reflection.

"Let me tell you another story," I said.

He regarded me with piercing eyes for a long moment and then nodded in resignation.

The Date

We stood looking at each other, in our creased suit pants and white shirts, our short hair and our business ties. Our black shoes shone brightly from their recent polishing. Elder Tanner grinned at me nervously and pulled my nametag off my shirt. I grinned back at him and pulled his off as well.

"Tonight we go out just as two men," he said. He took my hand. I could feel it trembling. He glanced at the front door. "Would you like to offer a prayer, Elder Smith?"

I nodded and bowed my head. "Dear Heavenly Father," I began, "please help us to have a good time tonight getting to know each other not as missionaries but as people. We ask this in the name of Jesus Christ. Amen."

It felt a little strange asking God for a blessing when we were about to break the rules. It wasn't as if going to a restaurant was a sin, of course. It was just that it wasn't Preparation Day, and we were supposed to be out working on Saturday night. Also, Mormon missionaries weren't supposed to date for the entire two years they were on their mission. Certainly not each other.

It was raining lightly, typical for springtime in Renton. I had enjoyed my last district in north Seattle, but I had to admit, the suburbs down south felt more like home back in Toledo. Elder Tanner was from Logan. It was the only piece of personal information I knew about him. As missionaries, we weren't supposed to talk about our former "civilian" lives. We were supposed to focus on missionary work.

We climbed in the car, Elder Tanner behind the wheel. He was the senior and always drove. He'd been in the mission field thirteen months, me just six. He was nineteen now. I was still eighteen. We'd been together a full two months, and I loved him more every day. He tended my foot for a week when I stepped on a nail. He traded chores with me that I didn't like, letting me get all the easy ones. He let me win at basketball at church on P-Day, the only thing that made the boring game bearable. He bought me a piece of cheesecake when an investigator turned on us last week and yelled at me.

Last night, he read me the Song of Solomon.

We drove from our apartment past Fred Meyer and Wal-Mart and the Ford dealership and pulled into the parking lot at Buddy's Steakhouse. When we stopped the car, neither of us got out. Elder Tanner grabbed my hand on the car seat and smiled. I smiled back. Both our hands were trembling now.

It was raining a little harder than earlier, so we ran across the asphalt to the door of the restaurant. Inside was a tiny waiting room with an empty bench. A stuffed goose was hanging from the ceiling. A stuffed wolf was facing out a window. From where we were, all we could see was its behind. Elder Tanner pointed and giggled.

We walked through another door just as a huge man and slightly smaller woman came out. He was wearing a T-shirt that said, "Don't tread on me." She was wearing a white blouse with a drop of barbecue sauce on it. I fingered my white shirt and frowned.

In the main restaurant, we were greeted by three teenage girls. "How many?" asked one perky little thing. Her T-shirt read, "Preciate Ya!"

"Two," said Elder Tanner.

"The wait is about twenty minutes. This will light up and vibrate when your table is ready." She handed my companion what looked like a huge cell phone and then brushed us aside as another couple walked in.

Elder Tanner nodded to me, and we headed back out to the waiting area and sat down on the bench. "I'm so happy to be here with you," he said.

"Elder, we eat together every night."

He punched me in the arm. "You know what I mean."

I put my hand on my stomach. "I have so many butterflies, I don't know if I'll be able to eat at all."

"We're going to have a *great* meal."

Two teenage girls came in with two teenage boys. The door slammed behind them as they walked into the restaurant. "So, Elder Tanner," I said nervously, wanting to get to the real date stuff, "what's your first name?"

He threw up his hands helplessly. "I knew this moment had to come sooner or later." He took a breath. "It's Felix."

"Felix?"

"I'm afraid so. It means happy."

"Gay?" I suggested, smiling.

He looked quickly toward the door to make sure no one had come into the waiting area. "Happy," he repeated with a fake frown, a twinkle in his eyes. "And you?"

"Billy."

"Not William, or Will?"

"Billy is written on my birth certificate."

He put his finger on his chin. "How do you feel about that?"

I shrugged. "I'll probably never be a CEO with a name like Billy, but that's okay."

Elder Tanner looked at me a moment. "It's odd, but I still want to call you Elder. That feels like your real name."

"I'm fine with putting that on our mailbox when we move to Capitol Hill after our missions." I grinned, and Elder Tanner looked nervously toward the doors again. A group of maybe eight thirteen-year-old girls and a couple of adults passed through the room. Two old people in their sixties walked out of the restaurant, followed a moment later by another heavyset man in his thirties and his heavyset wife, and a boy about six.

"I'm sorry," he said. "I'm just not used to this."

"Then maybe we should go on a date next Saturday, too."

Elder Tanner smiled. "We'll go on a date every Saturday for as long as we're still companions."

"How long do you think that'll be?"

"Don't know. Could be another week, or it could be four more months. As long as we keep our stats good, they'll leave us alone."

"Oh, I hope it's four more months. We'll have to work hard this week."

We chatted about our two investigators for a bit, and soon the device in Elder Tanner's hands lit up. He opened the door for me, and we went up to the perky girl again. She handed us off to another perky girl with repulsively tight pants, pointing out much too clearly that she did not have well-formed legs. Odd that she might think she looked sexy in that outfit.

A man in a suit looked sexy.

The girl in tight pants led us to a table in the middle of a vast room, handed us two menus, and set some cutlery wrapped in cloth napkins in front of us. Country music was playing softly, but the roar of the other diners was almost deafening. I hoped I'd be able to hear Elder Tanner talk. But I supposed it also meant no one would overhear us.

"What would you like to drink?" the girl asked after we sat down.

"Water," said Elder Tanner.

"Water," I said.

"We have several great beers," she pressed. She pointed to a page on the menu.

"Water," Elder Tanner repeated.

The girl nodded and headed off.

I looked at the menu. The steaks were expensive, from $18 to $23. This meal would put a huge dent in our budget. Maybe our next date should be at McDonalds. I looked over at Elder Tanner. Still, I was glad our first was going to be memorable. I was torn between two options on the menu, a T-bone for $22 or Fish and Chips for $13. Elder Tanner was paying, so I wondered if I should go with the Fish and Chips.

I'd been on several dates with girls since turning sixteen a couple of years ago. In retrospect, those all felt like going to a dance with my sister. Tonight felt like the real thing.

Was Heavenly Father going to punish us?

Elder Tanner closed his menu, and I closed mine. While we waited for the waitress to return, I noticed two older men at the table next to us, in their fifties. One of the men, wearing a goatee, was smiling at me with a bemused expression. I turned to look at the table beside the men. A couple in their thirties, both heavyset, were feeding a blond-haired boy about two, and a slightly older girl in a high chair. The girl looked listless. As I watched, the father pulled her out of the chair, and I could see a piece of plastic tubing hanging down from the girl's side.

Life wasn't fair.

Heavenly Father had put me in a church that condemned gays, but he'd also given me the love of my life.

Was that kind of him, or mean?

The perky girl with tight pants came back to our table. "Have you decided?" she asked, with her pen ready.

"I'll have the sirloin," said Elder Tanner, "medium rare, with a Caesar salad and a baked potato."

"Did you want anchovies with your salad?"

"Definitely not."

She turned to me. "I'll have the sirloin, too, medium well, though, with baked beans and sweet potato fries."

The girl left, and I looked at Elder Tanner. We'd done it. We'd ordered. We were officially on a date. I smiled at him and a moment later felt a hand on my knee under the table. I closed my eyes. Would we kiss later? I wanted him so badly, but we were still missionaries, after all.

"What do you want to be when you grow up?" asked Elder Tanner, squeezing my knee and removing his hand.

"An accountant," I replied. "I like numbers."

"Ugh, that sounds horrible." He laughed. "But my choice isn't much better. I want to be a UPS driver."

"Why is that bad?" I asked.

"It doesn't show any ambition."

"But you like to drive?"

He nodded. "I like being out and about. And lifting packages all day will keep me in shape."

"Then I don't see anything wrong with it."

"My father hates the idea. Says I'm a loser."

I saw the pain in his face and wanted to slap his father. "You could never be a loser."

Elder Tanner's eyes fell. "We're going to the Telestial Kingdom, aren't we?" he asked softly, hard to hear over the ruckus in the room. "Or to Outer Darkness."

"We're going to wait till we're married and living on Capitol Hill before we have sex," I replied. "Heavenly Father will just have to make allowances. You can only be as good as your situation permits. A diabetic can't fast."

Elder Tanner sighed and cracked open a roasted peanut from a little paper tray on our table filled with them. He ate the two peanuts inside and threw the shells on the floor. "I hope you're right."

"Elder Tanner, I love you. And that love doesn't feel evil. It's the best feeling I've ever had. Even better than the feeling I get when I bear my testimony. Loving you *can't* be wrong."

Elder Tanner looked at me and smiled, not a weary smile but a hopeful one. "I love you, too," he said.

"The Church'll come around."

"Do you really think so?"

"It *has* to. The Church is true. So it has to accept all truth. And the truth is that our loving each other is right."

I saw the man with the goatee at the next table motioning to the other man, who took a quick glance over his shoulder at us. Were they old gay letches ogling younger men, I wondered. Or did they recognize us because of our outfits? Maybe they were interested in hearing the lessons. As much as I wanted more investigators so that I could stay with Elder Tanner longer, I was irritated by their glances. Elder Tanner and I should have worn our P-Day clothes, even if it wasn't P-Day.

But we had an appointment at 8:00 with a member family and couldn't risk not being ready in time.

The father at the other table put a shoe on the little girl's foot. It had fallen to the floor. The girl seemed oblivious. The mother continued eating her fries. The little boy was playing with some kind of action figure.

Three servers shouted a fast-paced happy birthday song and brought what looked like a sundae to a table near us.

"Elder Smith, tell me something else about you that I don't know."

I thought for a moment. I wasn't terribly interesting, but like any young man, I suppose, I felt the need to impress my date. "I used to volunteer at the animal shelter," I said. "We killed most of the animals, but I wanted them to be as happy and comfortable as they could be in their last days."

"I want to know more."

"I like reading Agatha Christie," I continued. "I like homegrown tomatoes and like growing them myself. I'm handy with gardening. I like gargoyles. I hate sports, but I want to train to run a marathon one day."

Our server brought our meals then, and I started eating my fries while Elder Tanner worked on his salad. I watched him eat. How could someone look so attractive when he was chewing?

"And you?" I asked, eating a spoonful of beans.

Elder Tanner looked thoughtful. "I hate reading. I hate tomatoes. I hate gardening. But I love sports, especially football."

"Excellent!" I said. "That means we'll always have time to ourselves and won't get on each other's nerves by being together all the time."

"I'm with you all the time now and love every minute of it."

Something about the way he said it made me feel hopeless, as if we were secretly spending money we'd found in a lost backpack on the sidewalk.

"I love grocery shopping with you," he went on. "I love cleaning the park every week with you when we do our community service. I love straightening up the apartment with you."

I wanted to massage his back, rub his chest, grab his penis through his pants. "I love spreading the Gospel with you," I said.

"Maybe we can be stake missionaries together after our missions."

The older man with the goatee was still looking at me every few minutes. What if he was a member and knew we had deliberately removed our nametags? We could get in trouble. We could get separated at the upcoming transfers next week. If we were still together next Saturday, maybe Elder Tanner and I should just have a special meal together alone in our apartment. That's what married couples in love did, wasn't it?

The little girl's shoe had fallen off again, and the father patiently returned it to her foot.

I began eating my steak. Elder Tanner and I talked about applying to attend the University of Washington after our missions. He would find an apartment here while I was still serving and get everything ready for my arrival. We'd be living on student loans and part-time jobs the first few years. But we were used to being poor. We lived out of two suitcases now.

We talked about high school. I had been president of the math club. Elder Tanner hadn't had the right build or skills to play football, but he attended every game. He almost tried out for cheerleading, but he was afraid that would give him away.

We talked about our pets, about our brothers and sisters, about our parents. We talked about the music we liked, our favorite movies. I was beginning to see a completely new person than the one I thought I knew.

I liked this one, too.

Elder Tanner continued to put his hand on mine underneath the table every few minutes as we ate and talk. The servers sang another happy birthday song to another couple. The family with the sick girl left, and a man with a cowboy hat and a woman wearing a tight T-shirt sat at their table.

I thought of Elder Tanner's crotch. Maybe Heavenly Father *should* separate us next week. We couldn't get married in the temple, but I still wanted to be a virgin when I got married.

How could this man look so attractive when he chewed?

I finished my steak, quite full, but still wanted dessert.

I wanted Elder Tanner.

Was this all just a hopeless dream? What if he forgot about me after transfers? What if he didn't move to Seattle after his mission as he said? What if tonight was all we had?

Would he still love me after we were excommunicated for each other?

I watched as the two middle-aged men got up from their table. They started to pass us on their way to the door. One of them, a little heavy, with a trim gray beard, leaned over when he reached our table. "Hi, Elders," he said, pointing to the other man with the goatee. "We served together in Madrid."

And then they were gone.

Elder Tanner and I looked at each other. Heavenly Father *approved*. It was a sign. We could grow old together. It was really possible. God had sent that other couple here tonight to show us. There really were miracles today like in olden days. The Church was true. I felt a burning in my chest and sent a prayer heavenward.

Elder Tanner took my hand on top of the table and smiled. I leaned over and kissed him.

I couldn't wait to go tracting with him in the morning.

The Hotel Room

"You are so adorably cute when you get excited," said Sefton as I finished my tale. "I'm enjoying watching you."

Good, I thought, since we still had a few hours yet to kill. My plan was working so far, but it was exhausting me emotionally. If I didn't perform well every single second, Sefton would grow tired of me and the evening would be over. He'd go home, get some sleep, and maybe still make that damned vote. For all I knew, this particular bill wouldn't come up in the morning as I'd originally assumed but in the middle of the afternoon instead. I needed to keep him awake absolutely as long as possible. After a few unhappy stories, I'd wanted to show him something more tender this time, hoping that would keep him interested longer.

He seemed to have liked it.

"Well, did you know you twitch your toes when *you* get excited?" I asked. I was learning to tell that when he was truly enjoying one of my stories, he wiggled his toes almost constantly.

Sefton laughed. "No one's ever noticed that before. You're very observant."

I ought to be, I thought, with all the projects and experiments I did at Georgetown. Right now, I was studying tumor invasion for my Immunology class. The project was wreaking havoc on my own immune system through fatigue and sleep deprivation. I hardly needed to add tonight's activities to the list. I was grateful no one person had to know everything in order to make a significant contribution to science. We each added a tiny bit to the overall body of knowledge.

Attempting to give Sefton a decade's worth of gay interactions in one night and cramming a whole course load of self-realization into a few hours was as impossible as completing my degree in a single semester. But if I could help Sefton truly connect with another gay man, perhaps it would make a difference in his life. Maybe he'd end up coming out five years from now instead of in ten.

I thought it sad that no one had ever noticed Sefton's wiggly toes before. I was always amazed at how little most other people observed around them. To me the biggest enjoyment in life was noticing things.

"I notice your eyes light up whenever I hold your hand," I said, caressing his fingertips.

"Now you're embarrassing me."

I tilted my head and gave him a long look, wondering. "What *was* the most embarrassing thing that ever happened to you?"

"Why in the world would I ever tell you that?"

"Because then you'll have nothing left to hide from me. We can be completely honest with each other." I massaged his palm. "I can tell you that the most irritating thing for me growing up was getting into trouble. My father would always say, 'Houston, we have a problem.' You don't know how old that can get." I exhaled a heavy breath. "Tell me something you've never told anyone else."

For a long moment, he looked at my hand resting in his, and then he gazed into my eyes. I noticed that he had more worry lines than laugh lines, and I wondered if it was already too late to work on this man. Some damage was too serious to repair. "On my honeymoon," he began slowly, "my wife and I were both virgins. Neither of us knew much about sex. My parents hadn't told me anything at all, and I never talked to my friends growing up because I could tell something was wrong with me, that I didn't like girls the way I was supposed to.

"So there we were in our hotel room, both nervous and embarrassed. I was sexually aroused just at the prospect of finally having sex, even with a woman. So I had a big hard-on. My wife insisted we do it in the dark, so there we were fumbling around, and I finally found her hole. She grunted in pain, but I was determined to prove I was a real man.

"So I thrust myself inside her and…"

"Yes?" I said softly, trying not to spook him.

"Then I urinated."

"What?"

Sefton covered his face and shook his head. "Not much. It's not easy to urinate when you have an erection. But I thought that's what you were *supposed* to do. I didn't know any better. When she realized what I'd done, she screamed and hit me. I was simply mortified. We didn't have sex again for the rest of our honeymoon.

"Ever since, whenever she's mad at me, I usually find out because she'll try to pee on me a little when we're having sex." He shook his head again. "And a few years ago, when she sensed I was growing distant and she feared I might have an affair, she threatened to tell the media about our honeymoon if I ever cheated on her."

"And would she still do that if she knew you were here with me tonight?"

"Probably."

"I'm sorry, Sefton," I said. "Your parents were jerks not to talk to you about sex."

"What is it about sex that makes people so afraid?" he asked.

"Why are *you* afraid?"

He slapped his forehead with the butt of his hand and grabbed his hair with his fingers. "I *want* to be normal. Normal straight. Even normal gay. Just normal. But we get so warped in life by our experiences. I can see it, but I can't do anything about it."

"Then you need better experiences." I kissed his elbow. "Let me tell you another story."

Home Teaching on Saturday Night

Chris mowed the lawn, the last time he'd probably have to do it for several months, as it was now mid-October in Seattle. Then he pulled out the big ladder and scooped the leaves out of all the rain gutters. He trimmed one bush that had grown too lanky over the summer. And he painted the columns on the front porch. Next weekend, he could paint the landing.

"Looks good, dear," said Cammie, sticking her head out with Babette in her arms. Babette was just one. The other girls, Melody, three, and Caitlin, five, were inside playing or watching TV.

"Thanks, honey," said Chris, walking over to the doorway to give Cammie a kiss. Babette reached for his face with one hand, and he gave the child a kiss, too, playfully rubbing his moustache against her nose. Babette giggled. "I'll be done in a few minutes."

"Oh, good. I need to get to the store to buy a few things. I'll bring Caitlin and Melody, but could you watch Babette? It's almost time for her nap anyway."

"No problem, sweetie." Chris watched as Cammie smiled and closed the door. They'd been married almost seven years now. Seven years. Chris had heard about the seven-year itch, but he'd been faithful to Cammie since Day One. Cammie was a Nursery leader at church, and Chris was second counselor in the Elders Quorum. He'd hoped for something a little more substantial by this point, but it was an easy enough job, teaching Priesthood one Sunday a month. Other than that, the only other real calling Chris had to worry about was Home Teaching. Four families in the ward were assigned to him, and with his junior companion Kevin, just fourteen, Chris met with all four families once each month. He was one of the few elders who did 100% of his Home Teaching, bringing the Elders Quorum average to almost 31%.

Chris and Cammie were still a young family. To be truly good Mormons, they still needed to have one or two more kids. In the old days, even four children would have been considered half a family, but these days, you could achieve the Celestial Kingdom with fewer children. Cammie hated being pregnant, but the good thing was that once pregnancy was achieved, she was no longer afraid of sex. Nothing else to lose. So she and Chris had sex regularly up until the end.

But days like today…

Even though it was a Saturday night, "date night," they probably wouldn't have sex. She wasn't ready for another nine months of nausea. Not even condoms could persuade her.

Chris put away the paint and washed the brush, and Cammie swished by with a quick kiss on her way to the car with the two older girls. Babette was asleep. Chris thought it an opportune moment to take a nap himself and relaxed on the sofa. He liked looking at their painting of the original Nauvoo temple on their wall. It was soothing and comforting. He also liked looking at their print of a glorious Jesus Christ descending from the clouds. He smiled and then closed his eyes. Not two minutes after Cammie drove off, though, there was a knock on the door. Chris hurried over to open it before a second knock awakened Babette.

"Hey, Burt," said Chris. It was his next door neighbor.

"Hi, Chris." Burt looked nervously over his shoulder and then into the house beyond Chris.

"What's up?" asked Chris.

Burt shrugged. "Gloria's out of town and I'm feeling a little lonely."

"Come on in," said Chris, motioning for Burt to follow him into the house. He shut the door behind his neighbor, and they walked to the living room and sat down on the sofa together. "So, Gloria's gone for the weekend, huh?"

"Yep, she's gone."

There was an awkward silence for a few moments. Then Burt tugged at the crotch of his pants for a second, as if the fabric was sticking too closely to his skin. He looked at Chris.

"Can I take care of that for you?" asked Chris.

Burt smiled, breathing a sigh of relief. "I get so horny when Gloria's out of town." He stood up and unzipped his pants, dropping them to his knees. He wasn't wearing underwear. Chris leaned forward and took Burt's penis in his mouth. It had a salty and slightly musty taste, as if the man hadn't washed yet today. "Stick your finger up my ass," Burt commanded. Chris licked one finger and pried it slowly into Burt's ass as he continued to suck the man's dick. Soon Burt was bucking back and forth and then thrust forward strongly as he came. Chris could feel the cum hitting the roof of his mouth.

He let the cum slide around on his tongue for a long moment, savoring the taste.

Burt put his dick back in his pants and zipped up. "Thanks, Buddy."

"Any time."

Chris showed Burt to the door and then went back to relax on the sofa again.

Chris helped Cammie put the handful of groceries away when she came home a short time later. He played Chutes and Ladders with Caitlin, let Melody ride piggyback for fifteen minutes, and when Babette awoke, he read a five-minute children's book to her about monkeys and sang a couple of children's songs. Cammie started working on dinner.

Chris left the girls to play by themselves and picked up his copy of *The Vitality of Mormonism* by James E. Talmage. He'd finished Thomas S. Monson's *Pathways to Perfection* last week. Chris always had chores on Saturday, but he liked to spend as much of his weekend as possible reading from the General Authorities. It made him feel…virile.

Around 4:45, maybe fifteen minutes before dinner would be ready, Chris went to take a walk around the block. Sometimes, he took the kids with him, but today, they seemed happy with each other, and Chris liked walking at an adult pace when he had the chance.

Seven years, he thought. Their anniversary was in three weeks. Chris had already bought Cammie her own personal set of temple clothes for the occasion, so they wouldn't have to rent every time they went to the temple over in Bellevue. He could hardly wait to see her face. He had also bought her a pretty green scarf, for use outside the temple. Chris would have liked to buy her expensive gifts, but with only one salary to pay for a family of five, he had to do the best he could.

One street over, a man was lifting a wingback chair out of a truck, struggling to get a good grip on it. Chris had seen the man before on other walks and occasionally exchanged a brief greeting, but they didn't really know each other. He'd thought the man looked at him even after Chris passed sometimes but wasn't sure. So he was a little surprised when the man motioned for him to approach. "Would you mind terribly?" the man asked, a little winded. "I just can't get it by myself. We only need to bring it into the living room."

"No problem." Chris grabbed one end of the chair and the man grabbed the other, and within two minutes, the chair was placed securely next to the sofa in the living room. It didn't match, but that wasn't really Chris's concern.

"Is there any way I can thank you?" asked the man, rubbing his hands as if touching the chair had made them dirty.

"No need," said Chris. "Happy to help."

"Well, let me do *something*," said the man, reaching forward and grasping Chris's hand.

"Like what?" Chris was puzzled as the man pulled on his hand, forcing Chris to follow him up the stairs and to the master bedroom. The man reached for Chris's buckle, unzipped his pants, and pulled them down to Chris's ankles. He tugged off Chris's shoes and then finished pulling off the pants. Then he pushed Chris onto the edge of the bed and lifted Chris's legs. He reached over for some lubricant on the bedside table, and a moment later, he was inside Chris.

It felt wonderful. The man slid forward and back, forward and back, and Chris could feel the tension on his sphincter. As the man neared climax several minutes later, he began pushing forward harder and harder. Finally, with a loud groan, he thrust forward and stopped moving, his head resting against Chris's foot. Chris imagined the man's cum inside his ass, wishing he could have felt it hit the walls of his rectum. He didn't want to move.

"Damn," said the man. "Now I've got to piss."

"Go ahead," Chris whispered.

The man's eyes widened in surprise, and then he smiled. His dick still inside Chris, he let go, and this time,

Chris could feel the liquid inside him. When the man finished, with a friendly grin, he pulled out and pointed Chris in the direction of the en suite bathroom. Chris picked up his pants and shoes and hurried off. After he finished in there, he went back out to the bedroom. The man had already dressed again, as had Chris. They shook hands, and the man led Chris to the door. He didn't even know the man's name.

Chris walked the rest of the way around the block and ended up back home just as Cammie was setting food on the table. It took two parents to control three young children at dinnertime, but Cammie talked about something Gloria had done the day before, Chris talked about something a coworker did, and dinner passed uneventfully. After Chris put the leftovers away and washed all the dishes, he joined the others in the family room.

"Who wants to watch a movie?" asked Chris, walking over to the DVD shelf.

"*The Little Mermaid*! *The Little Mermaid*!" both Caitlin and Melody shouted together.

Chris looked over at Cammie and laughed. Thank goodness Disney made shows worth seeing again and again. They'd probably seen this one twenty times at least. It wasn't like *The Secret Life of Walter Mitty* that Chris had gone to see on his own last Thursday night, telling Cammie he was doing Home Teaching. Sometimes, he just had to have some time to himself. It didn't mean he didn't love

Cammie and the kids. Cammie sometimes hired a babysitter and took afternoons for herself as well.

Chris might just have to go see that *Walter Mitty* movie again. There was something about it which appealed to him. He'd never cheated on Cammie, but fantasizing about it with the neighbors sometimes helped him get through the day. Men understood about sex. He thought about his boss at work calling him into his office and demanding that Chris give him a blow job, then discovering that he was so good at it that he had Chris service all his work buddies in the office and in nearby buildings downtown. Sometimes, Chris liked telling Cammie he was going Home Teaching, and then just driving around town looking at cute men. Sometimes, he fantasized about black men fucking him. Sometimes, he fantasized about Hispanic men fucking him. Sometimes, he fantasized about Asian men fucking him.

Then he'd come back home, and Cammie would say she wasn't interested in sex that night, and Chris would go in the bathroom and beat off into his hand, licking the cum off his palm. Hopefully, Cammie would relent soon, she'd get pregnant, and then Chris would have at least a few months of regular sex again. Of course, he and Cammie got along just fine even without the sex. She'd read her latest Deseret purchase to him in bed, and they'd talk about how wonderful it would be to make it to the Celestial Kingdom together. Sometimes, she'd recite her latest poem to Chris, and Chris would either praise it or suggest a minor change to improve it. Chris felt that Cammie almost preferred the latter, as it seemed to convince her that Chris was more fully engaged in what she was saying.

Chris was looking forward to their seventh anniversary. He'd already hired a sitter far in advance so there would be no mistake, and he was taking Cammie to her favorite Italian restaurant.

Sometimes, Chris fantasized about Italian men fucking him.

The movie was only half over, but Chris leaned over and whispered in Cammie's ears, "Home Teaching. Be back in a little while."

"Sometimes, I think you're too dedicated to the Church," she whispered back. But she was smiling.

He gave her a peck on the lips and then climbed in his car and drove off down the street. Tonight, he'd go past the video store he'd discovered in White Center a while back. He'd park outside and watch the men going in, hungry for satiation, and watch the men coming out, emptied and ready to head home. Maybe he'd see the East Indian man there again as he had a few weeks ago. He needed to memorize how the man looked so he could fantasize more clearly about him.

He rubbed his crotch and pressed on the gas, his Family Home Evening manual on the passenger seat beside him.

The Hotel Room

Sefton was staring at the floor when I finished. His toes were not twitching. "You okay?" I asked. I needed to make him uncomfortable if I wanted him to change, but it was a fine line I was walking.

"I'm such a bad father," he said listlessly. "My kids deserve better. Sometimes, I think I should kill myself so my wife can remarry."

"You haven't heard of divorce?"

"That would scar the children."

"And having a father hanging from a tree in the back yard wouldn't?" I asked.

"Oh, I wouldn't do it like that."

"Regardless."

"I wonder just how many men in the Church are living lives like this? So much lying and deceit."

"You know, there's an alternative to living a double life."

Sefton's eyes narrowed. "Don't go there."

"No one cares anymore."

"Yes, they do."

"You're a politician. Haven't you been paying attention to all the states that now allow gay marriage?"

"Even in Utah and Idaho," Sefton said wearily. "But we still know it's wrong."

I shrugged. "It's as if it were a crime to be blond-haired, and then suddenly no one cared any more what color hair you had. Being gay will eventually be just as unimportant. Nobody will think twice about it."

"My family would think twice." He sighed heavily.

"They'll get over it if they truly love you," I said.

"Well, that's the issue, isn't it? Sometimes families aren't all they're cracked up to be."

I thought carefully about what I wanted to say next. "Do you love your family?"

"You know," Sefton said, "I spend hardly any time with my children at all. I'm afraid to contaminate my two sons. But I don't even spend time with my daughters. Mormons are supposed to be so strong on family, but I make my wife take care of the kids all by herself. I provide the money, and she provides everything else. And of course the Church leaders set any other examples they need."

"Of course." I picked at a bit of dried semen on my thigh.

"I've read some articles that say homosexuality is genetic, but I've also seen a report that says even though *most* identical twins are either both straight or both gay, they aren't *all* like that. So it can't just be genetic. It has to be environmental. So I want to give my kids a good environment and stay away from them."

"Sefton, a kid can lead a perfectly happy life if he's gay. But he'll be screwed up for years if he thinks his father doesn't love him."

"I know, I know," he said wearily. "And what if it's the feeling that his father doesn't love him that makes him gay in the first place?"

"That's 1950's psychology. We're well past that now."

"But even you don't *know* what makes a person gay, do you?"

I shrugged. "No. But I know it's determined extremely early in a person's life. You may as well get close to your kids while you can. They're either gay or straight already, and nothing you can do about it now is going to change anything. No sense hurting both them and yourself by staying distant."

"I suppose you're right." He scratched at an itch on his knee, slowly at first, and then harder and harder, until it looked like his skin would bleed. "There are just so many things I want to do differently," he said through gritted teeth. "I'm not sure I can do everything I want to do."

"Well, I'm sure, Sefton. You can't. No one can. But that doesn't mean you shouldn't do *some* of them."

Sefton looked at me and nodded. Then he offered a faint smile. "I've so wanted to talk to a therapist, but I can't have that on my record. Thanks for really listening to me. You'd have made a good bishop if you'd stayed in the Church."

I wasn't sure that was the compliment he thought it was. "I think it's time for another story," I said, returning his smile, and wondering if I should really push the buttons I was about to push.

To Open the Eyes of the Blind

"Of course I'm a virgin," I said. "Isn't everyone at BYU a virgin?" I frowned. "Except for the married students, of course."

My branch president smiled at me, a bit condescendingly, I thought. "Even some of the saints are weak," he replied. "Particularly people like you."

I felt my armpits instantly grow wet. "What's wrong with me? Just because my father's a bishop?"

"You know what I'm talking about."

I did, but I was sure he couldn't really *know*. I'd never told anyone, never acted on my feelings even once. I was a good boy, and I'd be serving as a missionary as soon as my freshman year at Brigham Young University was completed.

"I—I don't even date," I said. "I don't want to leave a girlfriend behind for two years."

"Jeremy," said President Blakely softly, "I'm going to give you a recommend for electroshock therapy."

I felt the color drain from my face. "Wh-what? You mean like a temple recommend?"

"Of course. You can't go without a recommend." He chuckled. "BYU's been getting excellent results," he went on. "If you're really still a virgin, your chances are even better. Don't you *want* to get married and have a family? This is your only chance to overcome those homosexual feelings."

I felt sick. How had he guessed? I was a good-looking boy. At least, when I looked in the mirror, I thought *I'd* be attracted to me. And I had good friends. I wasn't a social misfit or anything. I volunteered as a math tutor. I cheered up the boys in my dorm who were homesick. I was fit, too, on the track team. And I'd been a Boy Scout, an Eagle.

"My father's a bishop," I repeated. "I have two brothers who served missions. My sister is married in the temple."

"But you're the youngest, aren't you?"

"Y-yes," I said in confusion.

"So you're the baby. You've been pampered. You've had it easy. And that's a key way for Satan to grab hold of your soul. But it'll be okay. The program really works."

"But President Blakely—"

"You're not going to sin and deny it, are you? Pride like that will make it much harder for Heavenly Father to help you. You *do* want to be cured, don't you?"

I stared at the floor. Was he going to tell my father? Would I be kicked out of school? Would they keep me from going on a mission? It was mortifying to talk about such a repulsive subject, but if this was truly my only chance, I decided I'd better take it.

"Yes, President, I want to be cured."

President Blakely slapped his desk. "Excellent!" His grin covered his entire face. "You'll meet with your therapist tomorrow at 1:00."

"I have classes at noon and 2:00."

"Exactly. You see, we're working with you. We want to help."

I nodded, and the president told me the details of the location on campus where I was to go the following day. I tried to smile. Then we prayed, he handed me the recommend, and I left. I strolled back to my dorm in a daze. It was early October, still warmer than I'd expected Utah to be. I was from San Diego, where it never grew cold. I missed my mother. I missed my dog. I missed my best friend, Scott, who'd gone to UCLA.

Life had been so easy back in San Diego. I belonged to the math club and the chess club and ran on the track team. That plus classes and Seminary and church kept me too busy to worry about my feelings. Whenever sexual urges became too insistent, I'd grab my father's lawnmower and walk around the neighborhood till I found a lawn that needed attention. People thought I was a great guy, so I'd had to repent of the deception every Sunday when I partook of the sacrament. Then I'd learned sign language on my own when a deaf 12-year-old girl was baptized three years ago, so I could interpret for her in meetings. That just made people think I had a crush on her, but despite the inappropriate age difference, I let them believe it. Being good always seemed to be tainted with some degree of sin.

I stood outside my dormitory, looking up at the building. It was just a few months since the Church had granted Blacks the right to hold the priesthood. There were big changes in the air. We'd defeated the Equal Rights Amendment, which would have brought destruction down on society. Maybe it was time to finally defeat homosexuality as well. This new science of electroshock therapy might be the modern advancement God had given the world to help save people like me, who might have been goners in an earlier time. I prayed, thanking Heavenly Father for giving my branch president the gift of perception so that he was able to call me out and offer the help I needed.

That night was a Fireside, on the subject of faith. I sat next to Doug, one of the guys in my student branch I really liked. We joked and laughed. I was determined not to let anyone else know my nasty secret. I'd be normal soon, and I could be true friends with people like Doug for the first time, without my sinful desires playing any role in it.

"How's the German coming along?" asked Doug after the talk was over.

"Wunderbar." I'd deliberately not studied Spanish because I didn't want to go to South America on my mission next year. I'd wanted to take French because I thought Paris would be lovely, yet with French there was always the chance of being sent to Canada, and that sounded too cold. German was pretty site-specific, and I really wanted to serve in Europe, despite the notoriously low baptism rates there. Of course, I knew that God had his own plans and I couldn't circumnavigate them, but I could do what I could to influence him. The Old Testament was full of stories of humans trying to persuade God.

Maybe if I worked hard and squashed my gay feelings, Heavenly Father would reward me.

"If it's going so well, why do you look depressed?"

"It's just a headache. I'm fine." I smiled brightly to prove it.

"Okay. See you at Family Home Evening tomorrow night."

I went back to my dorm, ignored my roommate Bill, who I thought very immature, and read the scriptures until bedtime. I never studied for school on Sundays.

I don't remember much about my classes the next day. My memory is all focused on the meeting with my therapist. After looking at the recommend the branch president had written for me, he had me sign a waiver stating that I did not hold BYU, the Church, or the therapist himself liable for any harm that might occur, or for any failure to become heterosexual. That failure would be entirely my responsibility, if I didn't exercise enough faith. I also had to promise never to discuss these sessions with anyone. As if I'd ever want to! I'd have rather died than let Doug or Scott or my family know what a terrible person I really was.

We established that we'd meet twice a week at first, on Mondays and Fridays. "Aversion therapy truly works," said Dr. Troutman. He never explained his credentials, so I assumed he was a psychologist or maybe a psychiatrist. "It helps people stop smoking, stop drinking, stop doing lots of negative behaviors that damage their lives."

"But I don't have any behavior to modify," I said. "I don't *do* anything gay."

"We don't use the word 'gay' here," said Dr. Troutman. "We say 'homosexual urges' or 'same-sex attraction.' These are degenerate feelings. We don't legitimize them by saying 'gay.'"

"Well, how are homosexual feelings a behavior?" I insisted.

"You're being very resistant. That's not a good sign. The fact is that you *choose* to think about men. And you masturbate, don't you?"

I felt my face grow warm. "Y-yes," I said. I jerked off maybe once a week. I wasn't sure if that was a lot or not since no one ever talked about these things, but I knew it was a wicked sin. I'd tried repenting for years, but I could never overcome the disgusting habit.

"And you think about men when you do it, right?"

"Yes," I mumbled.

"Those are choices. Those are actions. But this program will take care of all that."

That first day, he only attached electrodes to my hands and chest. I felt awkward sitting there without a shirt. Even though Dr. Troutman wasn't all that attractive, my semi-nude state made me feel sexual, and when I felt his fingers on my skin, I started to become aroused.

Thankfully, he turned off the lights then, and a series of slides began to show on a screen. I squinted my eyes at first. That looked like—oh, my god! Those were pictures of naked men! Naked men touching each other! I'd never looked at pornography before and couldn't believe what I was seeing. That man's dick—

Zap.

I jumped in my chair and shouted as a jolt of electricity passed through my body for a full three seconds. I wasn't sure I could say if it was painful or just uncomfortable, but it was certainly unpleasant. I looked away from the screen.

"No, you have to keep looking. We need to create an association in your brain. It'll take some time."

I kind of *wanted* to see the pictures, of course. Other than a few quick glimpses of nudity in gym classes or dormitory bathrooms, all I had was my imagination. It was kind of nice to finally see real men's bodies, doing what—

Zap.

I grunted and looked at Dr. Troutman. I was going to have to do this for two hours a week? How long would it take? Part of me felt grateful that it was suddenly acceptable for me to see these images. They were so nice, I was afraid the treatment might work too quickly and I'd lose my ability to appreciate their beauty. But I knew it was only an illusion of beauty, and it would bring me to Outer Darkness. Perhaps the program was working already. Did I still find that man on the screen attractive? His nipples—

Zap.

I groaned. Three seconds was a long time. "I don't want to do this anymore. It hurts."

"Excellent. We'll have you cured in no time."

"I want to go home."

"If you stop the sessions before you're cured, we'll have to declare a breach of the school's honor code."

I gripped the armrests on my chair and looked back at the next picture. That guy's blond hair was really cute, and that angular face—

Zap.

My eyes watered, and I blinked to clear my vision. I had to see the screen. I had to look at these men. Oh, my god. That man's dick was going into another man's ass. How could I be watching this at BYU? It was horrifying. And intriguing. And lovely. That man had a captivating hair pattern on his chest. And those arms alone were worth—

Zap.

I could smell burned hair, a nauseating odor, coming from my hands. I continued looking at the men before me, and I kept getting shocked, until 1:50, when Dr. Troutman pulled off all the electrodes and had me put my shirt back on.

"Great job," said Dr. Troutman. "You're progressing nicely."

I muddled through my next class and tried to study in the afternoon, but I found my mind kept wandering. I hoped the electricity wouldn't affect the regular activity of my neurons. Surely, that would only happen if they applied the electrodes directly to my head. Maybe we'd have to resort to that if nothing else worked.

I tried to assess my feelings. I didn't feel especially sexual right now. That was a good sign. What if I'd be normal in a few weeks? Maybe even in time for Christmas. What a wonderful present that would be. I couldn't even imagine how nice life must be for people who didn't carry this heavy burden around with them all the time.

Family Home Evening was in Doug's room. Everyone in our student branch divided up into small groups on Monday nights. It was only a substitute for a real family activity, but we didn't want to get out of the habit when we'd be forming our own families as soon as we came home from our missions. The family was not only the most important thing; it was really the *only* important thing. Everything else was secondary to supporting and promoting it. So every Monday, thousands of groups of students pretended to gather as families across the BYU campus.

"Hi, Jeremy," said Doug. "Boy, you look terrible. You have another headache?"

"Oh, I'm fine. Just a little eye strain. Thanks."

Norm, Doug's roommate, called everyone to order, and then he offered an opening prayer. "I thought we'd talk tonight about obedience," Norm went on after his prayer. "We're going to analyze Abraham's commitment to sacrificing Isaac, how we must do *anything* the Lord asks of us, no matter how difficult."

"What happened to your hand?" whispered Doug, poking me in the ribs and pointing.

"Burned it cooking," I whispered back.

"You have a stove?"

"Do you two mind?" said Norm.

I covered the burned spot on my hand with my other hand and concentrated on the lesson. These lessons never lasted very long. No one wanted a boring evening after a long day of classes. A few minutes later, just as we were wrapping up, Doug raised his hand.

"Yes?"

"Did you notice that after the attempted murder of Isaac, Isaac is never shown talking to his father again?"

There was silence in the room. I had certainly never noticed such a thing, but I spent more time reading the Book of Mormon than the Old Testament.

"So?" Norm finally responded.

Doug shrugged. "It just seems like we need to acknowledge that there are sometimes permanent unwanted consequences from following blindly."

"Well, we *accept* the consequences from obedience," Norm insisted. "It's the right thing to do. God will make everything better later."

"It's just that…"

"What?"

"It's just that I wonder if the test was really to make Abraham follow any commandment whatsoever, or if the test was to see if Abraham would challenge a truly unjust order."

Norm put his hand on his hip and stomped his foot.

"Remember the Nuremberg trials?" Doug went on. "When the Nazis said they were just following orders, they were told that didn't justify their actions."

"That's because they were taking orders from *men*," said Norm. "We're taking orders from God." His eyes narrowed and he added slowly, "So what commandment do *you* not want to follow?"

Everyone turned to look at Doug, even me.

He shrugged. "I don't particularly want to go on a mission," he said. "I'm planning on becoming a doctor. Maybe an ophthalmologist. It takes years of schooling. I don't want to get even further behind by taking off for two years."

Norm's lip curled. "Sounds selfish to me. We have to remember that if God gives us a commandment, there's a *reason*. Commandments are always for our own good."

I was still staring at Doug. He wanted to be an ophthalmologist? So did I. How come I didn't know this about him? I suddenly felt very close to Doug, and the idea briefly flashed across my mind that maybe this meant we were right for each other. Then I realized that another man could never be right for me. Besides, it had never occurred to me to worry about being two years behind the other medical students. Serving God on a mission was more important than being a doctor by the age of 26. Perhaps even a terrible sinner like me could show Doug how to see the importance of righteous priorities.

The meeting ended with a prayer from Ben, and then after a little isolated chatting, things broke up and people headed back to their own rooms. "Take care of that hand," said Doug, punching me lightly in the shoulder. "Burns can get infected."

I smiled weakly and nodded and then walked slowly out into the hall.

I was able to get back into my studies by the next day. On Wednesday night, I caught a glimpse of Doug getting into the shower at the end of the hall, and I locked myself in a bathroom cubicle and masturbated. I almost cried when I was done. I had desecrated my friendship with a truly good man. I prayed God would take pity on a sleaze like me and help me be cured quickly.

On Friday, it was all I could do to sit through my noon class. I was so anxious to continue my treatment and get better. I shook Dr. Troutman's hand firmly just after 1:00 and smiled. "I'm ready," I said.

"You'll need to take off all your clothes today," he said matter-of-factly.

I frowned but did as I was told. I felt very vulnerable standing naked in front of him but managed, thank goodness, not to get an erection. Dr. Troutman had me sit down, and he placed electrodes on my hands and chest as before, but he added one to my penis as well.

It was mortifying to be touched so intimately and know it was because I was thoroughly filthy. I wished he could hurry up and turn off the lights.

"Here's a dial," said Dr. Troutman. "You'll control the level of pain yourself."

I nodded.

I was amazed when the photos started flashing up on the screen by how accustomed I'd become to seeing nude men, after just one session. While the images still intrigued me, they also seemed perfectly normal and familiar. There was a Hispanic guy with a thick moustache. There was an Italian man with a throbbing penis. And there was—

Zzzt.

Whew.

Zzzt.

What was that?

Zzzt.

The electric shocks still lasted three seconds each, but now there was a series of ten in a row. After only the first series, I felt as if I'd just been beaten by a neighborhood bully. "What's going on?" I asked.

"Just keep looking. And remember, the level of pain you feel is up to you."

I looked back at the screen. A Black man was taking the penis of a blond man in his mouth. Oh, I'd wanted to do that for such a long time. Another blond with a beard was fondling himself. A dark-haired man was kissing another man.

Zzzt.

Zzzt.

Zzzt.

Zzzt.

My heart was racing, and I was sweating. But that penis up on the screen still looked like a work of art. I leaned over and turned up the dial a notch. I didn't know what to think. I *loved* looking at these pictures, but I so wanted *not* to love it. My eyes ate the screen hungrily, and I felt like scum for doing it. But just *look* at those arms, I thought, unable to turn away. And just look at that chest. And oh, my god, I had never dreamed a penis could be that beautiful.

Zzzt.

Zzzt.

Zzzt.

Zzzt.

I smelled burned hair again, and my penis hurt even when the shocks were no longer being administered. But as an athlete, I understood the saying, "No pain, no gain." I had a lot to gain here, so I knew it would require a great deal of pain. And I was ready to do what I had to do.

I was exhausted by the time the session was over. I had just one more burn on my hand and one now on my penis. But that was a small price to pay for spiritual freedom. I put my clothes back on, thanked Dr. Troutman for his help, and headed to my next class.

There was no dance or any other activity planned that weekend, so I didn't see Doug again until Sunday. "You look like shit," he whispered, sitting next to me in Elders Quorum. "Pardon the University of Utah language. Are you still getting those headaches? Maybe you should see a doctor."

"I'm okay. Thanks."

Doug put his hand on my arm. "I'm serious, Jeremy. Don't fool around with something like this."

I nodded and turned my attention to the teacher. "Today's lesson is on keeping pure," Malcolm began. The first time I'd seen him, I thought he was attractive, but I'd quickly found him to be annoying, and suddenly, he wasn't attractive anymore. I wondered how something unrelated to appearance could actually change my perception of that appearance. In a way, I was grateful. It was one less man to lust after. But there were times I tried to see him again the way I had that first day.

Men in general were creeps, though, so I didn't know why I didn't find fewer of them appealing. I wondered what role emotion had in my seeing males as attractive in the first place. How did my perceiving arrogance or spite in someone like Malcolm change the impulses hitting my eye's rods and cones? But if I could find this individual man attractive one day and ordinary the next, maybe my therapy sessions could help me see *all* men as unattractive before long. I wondered what part of perception I would have to alter, though, to see women sexually and men as uninteresting. Could electricity and pain really be all that was needed?

Malcolm's words were coming in and out of focus as I sometimes paid attention and other times let my mind wander, but at one point, he said something that grabbed me by the throat. "If thy right eye offend thee, pluck it out," he said.

I raised my hand hesitantly. "How does an eye offend?" I asked. "How can an eye sin?"

"Remember King David?" said Malcolm. "He looked at Bathsheba too long. And look at the problems that caused."

"So why didn't God tell *him* to pluck out his eye?" asked Doug. "And would plucking out just one eye do the job? Aren't we looking with both?"

"Well," said Malcolm slowly, "if you're really sinning a lot, you probably *should* pluck out both eyes."

There was some murmuring among the elders in the class. "Is that a real commandment?" asked Doug. "There would be a lot of blind Mormons running around if it was. And what about repentance? If you repent of having looked at something inappropriate, you're still blind the rest of your life. What shape would the Church Welfare program be in if 62% of Church members were blind?"

Malcolm sighed.

"And what about that next verse? If thy right hand offend thee, cut it off. How many guys in this room have ever beat off using their right hand?"

There was a stunned silence. People simply didn't talk about these things. Certainly not in church. But were we all thinking it? How could Doug know all the questions I was having myself, unless he was having them, too? Just how widespread was this type of grievous sin?

Malcolm gritted his teeth this time. "Doug, you always cause trouble. You know what the scriptures say about people who are learned."

"We're at BYU." Doug laughed. "We aren't supposed to use our brains?"

"Not to fight against God."

"Who's fighting against God?"

Malcolm closed his eyes.

"So if thy brain offend thee, get a lobotomy?"

I stood up and squeezed my way down the row till I reached the aisle, and then I hurried out the door. I felt sick to my stomach. Was my only hope of not lusting after men in photographs, or after men I saw on the street, to pluck out my own eyes? When I was in bed at night with my eyes closed, I could still see men in my mind. So did I need to cut off my hands? Castrate myself? Undergo an actual lobotomy like Doug said? If it was my spirit itself that was an offense, did I need to "pluck out" my very soul? Was committing suicide the only solution?

The next day, I had Dr. Troutman place two electrodes on my penis instead of just the one, and another on my testicles, plus the usual devices on my hands and chest. I turned up the dial as high as it would go.

"Are you sure?" asked Dr. Troutman. "We can work up to that level if we have to. But maybe you can be cured without such drastic measures."

Drastic measures? Was *anything* drastic if it kept a person from being cast into Outer Darkness? The Church obviously approved of this program, so the only thing for me to do was embrace it fully.

I stared at the first picture on the screen. It was of an Asian man who was flaccid. I was still flaccid myself. The whole idea of looking at men almost made me sick to my stomach. But that didn't mean I wasn't still fully attracted to them, that I didn't still want to—

Zzzt.

Zap.

Ssst.

Zzzk.

A dark-haired man with a thick chestful of hair held his hard penis like a weapon. A sandy-haired man also showed a lovely chestful of hair, and a wonderful bush of pubic hair as well. I gripped the armrests tightly, trying not to cry. *Why* did I want these men? What if even six months of loathsome sessions like this didn't cure me? What if I fell before I was healed? I could see Scott up on that screen. I could see Doug. I wanted to turn the dial even beyond its highest mark. It was what God wanted. The Church said so. I blinked my eyes dry and stared at the screen. The curve on that penis—

Zzzt.

Zap.

Ssst.

Zzzk.

I smelled burned hair again, and maybe even burned flesh this time. I wondered what the Jews in Auschwitz thought when they smelled that horrid odor coming from the ovens. Thank goodness Heavenly Father took better care of his *real* chosen people than that. God was helping me. He'd sent me to Dr. Troutman. I'd be normal soon. I would. By the time I got off my mission, that deaf girl would be old enough to marry. I kept staring at the screen.

There was a knock at the door. I barely noticed, luxuriating in the pain searing my body. Last night, I'd dreamed I was being executed in an electric chair, waking up disappointed it was only a dream. The knocking continued, becoming insistent, and Dr. Troutman turned off the electric shock machine and flipped off the projector.

"Hang on," he said in an irritated voice. "Must be one of the other subjects, but I tell everyone there's no dropping by."

My thoughts were still flying everywhere, but I was stunned to attention by that last comment. Just how many of us were there on campus? How many of us were there in the Church? Was there a Church-wide program of inflicting pain on people? Was this a pilot program?

Part of me thought about the huge advances that could be made if everyone were electrocuted into being righteous. But another part of me remembered that it was Satan's plan to force obedience rather than let people choose. Yet homosexuality wasn't a choice to begin with, no matter what my branch president said, so perhaps it didn't count. The ends might justify the means in this case.

Still, if I couldn't just snap my fingers and be normal, was it possible to do so by simply flipping a switch?

I wished Dr. Troutman would come back.

I heard the sound of arguing and turned. My mouth fell open when I saw Doug pushing his way past Dr. Troutman. Oh, my god. Was he a patient, too?

"Jeremy," said Doug, kneeling beside me. He looked as awful as I felt. It must be true then.

"I went to talk to your roommate, Bill." Doug was pulling electrodes off of my arms and chest. For some reason, I didn't feel naked in front of him. "He told me some things you were saying in your sleep, and I tracked you down." Doug carefully pulled off an electrode attached to my penis. "Jeremy, you're burned. You're coming back to my room so we can take care of that."

"But…but I need treatment," I said. "I can't leave. And I have a class at two…"

Doug stopped, his hand resting on the second electrode on my penis. "Haven't you ever seen *A Clockwork Orange*?" he asked.

I shook my head dully. "It's rated R."

"Look, they're not going to let you stay at BYU. Is there a school in California you could attend?"

I thought of Scott at UCLA. "Will they let *you* stay?" I asked.

Doug pulled off the last electrode on my penis and grabbed the one on my sac. He was almost vicious as he tore them off. "Yes," he said harshly. "I'm a *good* boy."

So was I, I thought. Then I looked at the blank screen and the machine sitting next to me. I saw Dr. Troutman off to the side on the phone, sounding angry.

"But…don't you believe?" I asked. "Why did you stop them?"

Doug had me stand up and handed me my underwear. "I believe that what God wants and what people *think* he wants are not always the same thing."

"Would you want to go to UCLA?" I asked. I suddenly felt very alone.

Doug laughed. "I don't want to be a missionary," he said, "but I do have a mission."

"What's that?" I pulled on my slacks.

"To open the eyes of the blind." He smiled, handing me my shirt. "Let's get out of here."

Dr. Troutman was off the phone then. "We'll be reporting you for breaking the Honor Code," he said to me in a rather cold voice. "I'd report you, too, if I knew who you were."

We hurried out before campus security could arrive, and Doug gave my arm a squeeze and headed off in another direction so we wouldn't be found together.

I wasn't sure why, but I knew quite fully that I wouldn't be going back for any more sessions. Was it simply because Doug's brief touch had felt so comforting? My perception of the world had changed in the blink of an eye. Somehow, I felt better, even understanding now I'd always be gay. Maybe liking men really wasn't the end of the world, after all.

That idea might still take a little prayer.

It would be a shame to lose all the tuition for this quarter, I thought, but in the long run, UCLA would be cheaper. Dad might not help pay for any school besides BYU, of course, but I could always take out a student loan and do work study on campus tutoring deaf students. The future was starting to look very different, as if I'd just taken off dark sunglasses and could now see my surroundings unshadowed for the first time. I had the bizarre impression that I truly was seeing colors I'd never seen before. I felt a little disoriented.

I suddenly had to pee, so as soon as I made it back to my dormitory, I headed for the bathroom. I stood at the urinal, looking down at my burned penis, and let out a stream. A moment later, someone stood beside me at the urinal, and when I glanced over, he smiled.

I nodded and then looked down to see his penis. I simply knew somehow I wasn't sinning. Well, I was pretty sure, anyway. The guy's penis twitched a little as I watched. Maybe I should be a urologist instead of an ophthalmologist, I thought. God did say he would help turn our weaknesses into strengths. I smiled, and I could see the guy thought I was smiling at him. I zipped up and thought about waiting till he was done, but I'd agreed to meet Doug, and my burns did need some care.

I looked at the man's back longingly for a second. Men truly were beautiful, I thought. I was glad I could really see that. I smiled again for a moment, and then I washed my hands thoroughly and headed out of the bathroom and down the hall toward Doug's room.

The Hotel Room

"Oh, my stars!" said Sefton when I stopped speaking. "What are you doing to me? You're killing me!"

"Didn't you like the story?" I asked carefully. Maybe I'd pushed too much.

Sefton sat on the edge of the bed, his legs hanging over the side, elbows on his thighs, his head propped on his hands. He glanced at me cautiously. "We really shouldn't be talking about this, you being an apostate and all."

"Yes?"

"My stake president prayed and was inspired to tell me how to treat my homosexuality. He told me to hit myself hard in the balls with a triple combination every time I masturbated while thinking of men."

I was so disgusted I wanted to puke, as I'm sure Sefton almost did every time he'd heeded the advice. Three volumes of scripture together could be pretty heavy.

I wasn't entirely sure it was a good thing that my story had struck so close to home. I was trying a sneak attack. Perhaps a direct confrontation would do more harm than good.

Sefton had let the evening go on longer than he'd planned, putting up almost no resistance. I seemed to be winning this game too easily, I thought. Then I started to wonder if maybe he *wanted* to lose.

Still, I'd seen it before. People heard all the logical arguments on a given topic, and they would agree with each point along the way. But in the end, they still acted out of a superstitious worry or some other illogical emotion. No matter how successful I felt I was tonight, I wouldn't really know if I'd made any progress till I watched the news the following evening.

"Do you feel your life *has* to be unhappy?" I asked. "That you have to make others around you unhappy, too?"

He buried his face in his hands. "That's not what I want," I heard his muffled voice say wearily.

"No one's forcing you to do it," I pointed out.

"I have to obey the commandments."

"At the cost of doing so much harm?" I thought of Derrick, but it was clear that lives could be destroyed even if they weren't actually snuffed out. I put my hand on Sefton's back. "Have you ever heard of the term 'chosen family'?" I asked.

"What's that?"

"Lots of gay people, and really, they don't have to be gay, anyone can do this, lots of people have found that their biological families have let them down. So they develop a truly strong circle of friends. I've seen friends there for each other for more years than married couples stay together. I've seen friends there for each other through losing a job, through losing a home to fire or foreclosure, through sickness, through almost anything."

Sefton looked at me in wonder. I'd seen the same expression on the face of a little boy in the news who'd been born deaf and had his hearing restored at the age of three, finally hearing his mother's voice for the first time— a look of absolute astonishment. Sefton shook his head slowly. "This idea that you can actually *choose* the people you want to share your life with, that you're not just stuck with people because they're related. I…I don't know if I could do a thing like that."

"Isn't it better than putting up with Uncle Charlie at every holiday gathering?" I asked.

Sefton looked wistful, and I wasn't sure how to read that. "Something about putting up with people you don't really like because you have to sounds noble," he said. "But something about surrounding yourself with people you truly enjoy being around sounds…"

"Yes?"

"Liberating."

"You do have a choice in the matter," I said. Sefton turned to me and frowned.

We were silent for several moments then. I was running out of steam and wondering how I was going to keep this up for another couple of hours. I wanted to keep our dialogue going a bit longer because that seemed somehow easier to sustain than inventing yet another story. But as I struggled for something else to say, Sefton continued the conversation himself. "You know," he said, "stories are powerful. Whenever there's a gun control bill or a bill to cut Medicare or a bill to support the oil companies, we hear stories. People who are affected one way or another come to the Senate and tell their stories."

"If they're so powerful," I said, "why do senators keep voting the wrong way so often?"

Sefton shrugged. "The Republican Party has become very ideological. In some ways, I think that's good. It keeps us focused." He paused. "But in other ways, it's made us blind." He laughed. "I can *see* that we're blind."

"So why don't you come over to the good side?" I asked.

"Democrats are sometimes big jerks, too," he returned. "I don't know that there are more than five or six good politicians out there from *any* party."

"So why not be the seventh?" I asked.

He looked at me strangely. "Do you ever watch reality shows?"

"As little as possible."

"There's this one about several people each vying to become a great chef. They put up with a horrendous boss who yells and curses and belittles them at every turn. And why do they put up with it? Because they *want* to be a great chef."

"Uh-huh."

"And there's this show about several young women who each want to be a supermodel. Same scenario. They put up with all this crap every week, week after week. You see them crying they're so upset. And why do they put up with it? Because they *want* to be a famous model."

"Okay," I said, almost amused at how gay his choice of programming seemed. "I see what you're getting at. But it's not the same. If people want to sell their souls to have their dream jobs, they're the only losers. Or winners. The outcome only affects them. But when a politician sells his soul…"

Sefton held up his hand. "What is *your* career goal?" He touched my cheek. "Gee, after all this time, I haven't asked that yet. I'm sorry. What *is* your goal in life?"

"I want to help cure cancer." I was a little nervous about saying it. If a client knew too much about me, he could really cause trouble. Georgetown was a Catholic school, after all.

"So why are you escorting?"

"To pay my tuition."

"So aren't you selling your soul, too?" he asked with a triumphant tone. "To achieve your goal?"

I shook my head. "No. I'm selling my body. Not even that. I'm selling my time. And my actions. And since I don't believe sex is a sin, I'm not betraying my own values." Not that I didn't still recognize the threat of danger in my behavior. There was always the possibility I'd be beaten up some evening, or end up with someone who wanted to kill me. Of course, there were times when I wished for such a confrontation.

Sefton crossed his arms over his chest. "And you think I am?" I heard both hurt and anger in his tone. Part of me wanted to let him win, so I could go on with my storytelling and keep him here longer, but another part of me wanted to truly win him over. All my experience with right-wingers told me I was wasting my time, but I was irritated.

"There were Jews assigned to be *kapos* in the concentration camps," I said, climbing out of bed and pacing the floor. "They had power over the other Jews. And they got better food and better treatment. You don't think they were selling their souls to do that?"

"They stayed alive, didn't they?"

"Actually, most of them didn't. They might have lived a slightly less torturous life for a while, but in the end, we all have to meet God. Is it worth being a *kapo* in a concentration camp just to meet God a few months later than you might have otherwise?"

Sefton threw up his hands. "Don't talk about God! I know I'm a terrible sinner. But not for my votes. I'm a terrible sinner for being here with you!" He covered his face with his hands, and I knew I'd blown it. He was going to kick me out, report to the Senate bright and early, no matter how sleepy he was, and vote against gays to prove to himself and to me that he was right.

I thought I had a hard life. I was trying to get through without the two people I loved most in the world. The project I'd just done a few weeks ago on molecular cytogenetics had wiped me out. I was studying every second I wasn't working. It was *hard*. But looking at Sefton, I realized there were people, even people with money and power, who were suffering a lot more than I was.

Sitting down beside him, I put my arm around his shoulder. "It's okay, Sefton," I cooed into his ear. "It's okay."

"It's not."

"It'll be all right."

"It won't."

We lay back down, and this time, I placed his head on my chest for a change. "There's something I want you to hear," I said.

"Oh, Matt," he said wearily. "I mean, Houston."

"You'll like this story," I said softly. I took a deep breath and began.

A Penis for Your Thoughts

Billy had recently turned twelve and was now asking us to call him Bill. I had ordained him to the Aaronic Priesthood and conferred upon him the office of deacon. He was taking it seriously, passing the sacrament every Sunday and coming along with me to collect fast offerings. Yesterday, he'd asked the question I'd been dreading: "Dad, is the Church okay with you holding the priesthood?"

I'd asked my bishop that very question twenty years ago, just before I married Constance. He'd ranted and raved and threatened to prevent our temple wedding and have me excommunicated.

But a streak of luck—Divine Providence?—had the man and his family transferred to another state before anything became of his threats. I married Constance, and after several years of sexual negotiating, we had Billy.

I mean Bill.

"I'm going to have to tell the bishop," I told Constance tonight as we climbed into bed.

She knew immediately what I was talking about. "Are you sure that's wise?" she asked. "Last time…"

"I have to know that Bill is truly a deacon," I explained. "I have to know when I ordain him a teacher, when I ordain him a priest, when I ordain him an elder, that he really holds the priesthood."

"You're in the Elders Quorum," she replied. "Of course you hold the priesthood."

"That's not good enough. I have to *know*."

She fluffed up her pillow and lay down facing me. "This affects me, too, you know. They'll hear the whole story."

"They'll find out anyway," I said. "How long do you think it will be before Bill says something? It's a miracle we've been able to put it off this long."

"But he's at such a vulnerable age. He might leave the Church if we get excommunicated."

I grasped the lace around the wrist on my nightgown. "And what about this?" I tugged at it firmly.

"Don't!" said Constance. "I love your frilly nightgown."

"And my wig?"

"Yes."

"And my women's garments?" Constance bought the sacred underwear through the Church. No one ever questioned why she continually ordered two separate women's sizes.

"And I love your bunny slippers, too. We've been through all this. You're the perfect woman for me. I wish you had breasts sometimes, but you're the sweetest woman I know, and I love you."

She leaned over to kiss me, and I let my lips linger on hers for a long moment. I wasn't a lesbian as she was, so Constance wasn't exactly the perfect fit for me, but she was the perfect friend, the perfect helpmeet, and the perfect sister, though perhaps that turned our lovemaking into incest. Another thing to worry about.

I slept fitfully, and as soon as I arrived at work the next morning, I called the bishop at his pest control company. "Hello," he said. "This is Jim Barnes. We kill what's bugging you."

"Bishop Barnes," I replied. "This is Leon Cardiff."

"Brother Cardiff, what can I do for you?"

"I need to make an appointment. Do you have any openings tonight at the meetinghouse?"

There was a pause and some shuffling of papers. "Yes, I believe so. I have a 7:30. Will that do?"

"It's perfect, Bishop."

"I'll see you then, Leon."

"Thanks." I couldn't keep the despair out of my voice.

"Leon, it'll be okay," said the bishop softly.

"That's only because you don't know yet."

"It'll be okay."

Bishop Barnes had helped Constance with her doubts when she had breast cancer. He didn't realize that the best help came when she realized if I could be a woman without breasts, then she could, too. But he'd helped.

And he'd helped when I caught Billy—Bill—jacking off into a pair of my frilly lavender undies. I wore my garments most days. But on date nights, Constance and I both tried to dress sexy for each other, so we shared a drawer for those occasions.

But both of those events were more or less ordinary crises.

I wanted to see Bill go on a mission. I wanted to attend his temple wedding. I wanted to raise Bill in righteousness and watch him raise his own children in righteousness. I didn't want to be excommunicated.

But how long could I as a "righteous" man live a lie? How long could I do it as a righteous woman?

Dinner was a little quiet that evening. Bill ate quickly and asked to be excused. Constance said, "When is your appointment?" I hadn't even told her I'd called the bishop.

"7:30."

"I'll have dessert ready when you get home."

I looked at her and felt a lump in my throat.

She smiled and put her hand on mine.

At the ward meetinghouse, I went in at 7:28, not wanting to have to chat with anyone I might meet while waiting. Right at 7:30, the bishop ushered me into his office. He sat down behind his dark cherry desk, and I sat in front on a small padded chair. I looked at the floor.

"So, Brother Cardiff, what brings you to my office tonight?" asked the bishop in a cheerful voice.

I continued to look at the floor.

"Come, come, it can't be that bad."

"Is excommunication bad?" I mumbled.

"No one's going to be excommunicated," said the bishop soothingly. "Just tell me what's bothering you."

"I'm forty-two," I said. "I've held the priesthood for thirty years."

"Yes?"

"Bishop, I'm a woman," I blurted out. "I've felt so terribly guilty all these years, offering prayers and blessings when I have no right to hold the priesthood."

The bishop chuckled. "Is that all?" He laughed again. "You had me worried."

"But Bishop, I'm a woman—"

"Do you have a penis?"

"Yes."

"That's what counts."

"But I'm a woman, Bishop, with or without a penis. I wear wigs and dresses and nightgowns at home. I wear make-up. I wear women's garments. I'm a woman. I'm really a woman. Really."

"How does Constance feel about it?"

I shrugged. "She's a lesbian. She's fine with it."

"And you have a fine son," said the bishop. "Who's already told me some of this in our confidential interviews." He smiled at me calmly. "So what seems to be the problem?"

"Women can't hold the priesthood!" I almost shouted.

Bishop Barnes looked at me for a long moment, and I thought maybe I'd finally gotten through to him. Then he said slowly, "If Heavenly Father didn't want you to hold the priesthood, he wouldn't have given you a penis. He must *want* you to hold the priesthood."

"But—"

"Just go with the flow, Leon." He paused. "Would you rather I call you something else in private?"

"Leona," I mumbled.

The bishop smiled. "Leona. If that's all, I need to prepare for my next interview."

"Bishop," I said, "at the very least, will you talk to the stake president about it? See what he thinks?"

The bishop nodded thoughtfully. "Actually, I have a meeting with him tomorrow night. I'll talk to him about it then," he promised. "But I'm telling you, you have nothing to worry about."

Back home, Constance hugged me at the door. "Oh, dear," she said, seeing the look on my face. "It didn't go well? I was afraid of that."

I shrugged. "The bishop was perfectly okay with it. Said everything was fine."

"Then why are you so depressed?"

"Because he's wrong!"

"He's our priesthood leader. We have to sustain him."

I sat down at the kitchen table, and Constance brought over some poppy seed cake with powdered sugar frosting.

That night, I made love to Constance. She didn't much care for my penis, but she loved when I went down on her. In return, she dildoed me, which always made me feel properly under the control of a man.

I woke up the next morning feeling better, and as Wednesday passed and then Thursday, I began to feel that life might be worth living again. On my lunch break, I bought two pretty bracelets, one for me and one for Constance. She was a lipstick lesbian, after all.

Friday when I got home from work, Constance handed me a note. "The stake president called," she said solemnly. "Wants to see you at the stake center tonight at 7:00. We'll have to hurry dinner."

"I'm not hungry."

Bill came in the kitchen and I asked about his day before he wandered back to the living room. I looked at him, so masculine and strong, even at twelve. Then I looked back at Constance, who was biting her lip. I sighed.

So Bishop Barnes had talked to the stake president, after all. And a higher authority had seen things more clearly. It was devastating, of course, but a relief as well. Maybe now I could start wearing dresses in the daytime, too. What else did I have to lose?

I drank a glass of milk and then went in the bedroom to change. Standing in front of the mirror undressed, I fondled myself and tried to get turned on by the man I saw in the reflection.

All I saw was an ugly woman.

Constance and I were legally married. They couldn't keep us from attending church together as two women. I'd finally be able to attend Relief Society. Finally get to offer a class in Personal Enrichment. Finally get to be a Visiting Teacher.

It had to be better than being a Home Teacher.

But would they let me hold any callings at all? Even the lowly callings that a woman could hold?

I pulled into the parking lot at 6:50 and wished I had a cigarette. I'd never smoked, but it seemed like the thing to do under such circumstances. I paced up and down the sidewalk until 6:58 and then went inside the building. I found the stake president's office and knocked on the door.

"Come in, come in, Brother Cardiff," said President Turner warmly, ushering me in.

I went inside, but the moment I sat down, I decided to speak my mind. "There's no reason a woman shouldn't be able to hold the priesthood," I stated flatly.

President Turner laughed. "Oh, let's not go there tonight," he said. "I have something else I want to talk to you about."

I frowned, completely baffled.

"I've talked to Bishop Barnes. You know we've been needing to release his second counselor for some time now. The commitment is unfortunately hurting his work and family. But we think you're the right man for the job." He smiled broadly. "What do you think? Would you like to be Second Counselor in the Bishopric?"

I got a hard-on right there and then. "I'll talk it over with my wife," I said calmly, adjusting my pants, "and I'll pray about it. Can I give you an answer on Sunday?"

President Turner reached over to shake my hand. "We'll make you a High Priest, naturally. But we can take care of all the formalities later. You go home and have a good night's sleep on it."

That night, while licking labia as I fingered my frilly panties, I told Constance about my new calling. She moaned in pleasure and reached over to pick up the dildo.

The Hotel Room

"You really are going to keep me here all night, aren't you?" asked Sefton when I finished. I noticed his toes were twitching. I'd hoped that a little transgender diversion would cheer him up, though I realized it could also open up another whole can of worms.

"I want you to get your money's worth."

"Sheesh, I may pay you more to let me leave."

I stood up and pulled Sefton to his feet as well. "Let's do a few stretches," I said. "Get our blood pumping again."

Sefton smiled and we both reached for the ceiling together and then for our toes. We reached to the right and reached to the left. "I'm really enjoying your company," said Sefton.

He often didn't appear to be, and yet he was in fact still here with me. "And I'm enjoying yours," I replied honestly. I wanted to hate him for his hypocrisy and the harm he was doing to the gay community, but I was finding I actually liked the guy.

Then I remembered how Hitler's secretary had said that he was likable, too. Personality wasn't all that mattered. Actions mattered, too. I had to find a way to get through to Sefton.

We stretched for a couple more minutes and then sat down on the edge of the bed again. "You seem so positive about everything," he said. "It's fun to see. Senators are nothing if not negative."

"That's why you guys so rarely ever accomplish anything. You have to be positive to get results."

"And are you going to get results in cancer research? Are you going to win the Nobel Prize?"

Suddenly, I sensed the energy I'd been feeling all evening drain right out of me. "I honestly don't know," I said. "I was thirteen when my mother was diagnosed with ovarian cancer. She was trying to get pregnant and have a girl. She liked me and my brother, but she wanted a girl, too. When she went to the doctor to find out why she couldn't conceive, she learned she had six months to live."

"That must have been very difficult for all of you."

"I wanted to tell my mother *I'd* be her girl. I already knew I was gay by that point, but I was afraid to tell her. She died never knowing. I felt as if she died not knowing *me*. Sexual orientation is just one aspect of someone's personality, but it feels so significant that I felt I'd hidden the true me from my Mom, and when she died, I vowed I'd never hide my authentic self from anyone I loved ever again.

"I ended up coming out to my father two weeks after the funeral. In hindsight, I realize that wasn't perhaps the best timing, but my Dad handled it just fine. The only way

I felt I could make it up to my mother was to help other people with cancer."

"That's not a bad way to atone."

I shrugged. "It's just that as smart as I sometimes think I am, I'm always afraid I'm not smart *enough.* As hard as I work, I'm afraid I don't work hard *enough.*"

Sefton nodded. "That sounds like me every day of my life. Maybe we aren't so different after all."

"It's a hard worry to bear," I said. "I just don't see how you can handle that *and* a big secret at the same time. My load *has* to be lighter than yours."

Sefton looked at his hands. "What would it be like?" he asked softly. "What would it be like not to have this weight on my chest all the time?" He lifted his right leg and pointed to his foot. "Sometimes, I run with Velcroed weights on my ankles. I run several miles that way, and when I take the weights off, I feel like I'm walking on air."

"You ought to really think about taking the weights off your whole life," I said. He gazed at me as if hoping to find an answer in my face. I smiled and said, "It's time for another story."

The Sneakover Prince

I met Alan at the Faubourg Marigny gay bookstore in New Orleans. "Any new porn?" I asked breezily, walking past the counter where he was reading a book, and heading to the porn rack in back of the store.

"Oh, I—I don't know," he said. "I don't put out the magazines. I just work the cash register."

He actually sounded kind of nervous, as if talking about gay porn unsettled him. I smiled. How could you work in a gay bookstore and be uncomfortable with gay porn?

Well, he was new here, I figured. I hadn't seen him in the bookstore before. Still, even to come in and talk to the owner about a job suggested some degree of comfort.

I decided to test my suspicions about his jitteriness, just for fun. After looking through the magazines, I brought two up to the counter. One was the mainstream *Advocate Men* and the other was *Leather Men*. I put the two magazines in front of the new cashier and opened both, one to a photo of a businessman in an office with his pants down, and the other to a photo of a man in leather chaps kneeling doggie-style while another man in a leather harness rimmed him.

"Which do you think I should give my Dad for his birthday?"

The man became bright red in seconds and turned quickly to fiddle with some papers. "Is—is your Dad really gay?"

"Well," I said, "since the stroke, he can't remember, so I keep trying to convince him he is."

The man turned to look at me a moment, trying to figure out if I was joking or not. We chatted for about fifteen minutes. He told me his name was Alan, and he was working part-time here and part-time in a used book store in the French Quarter a few blocks away.

"Nice," I said. "I'm a librarian at Tulane University. We'll have to get together to talk about books sometime."

Alan looked a little flustered at that, but I wrote down my address and phone number and told him to give me a call or just drop by after work some day.

I didn't expect anything to come of it, but I was in the habit of regularly asking strange men over to my place, so I didn't see any reason to neglect this particular young man.

Only he wasn't really young, was he? He *seemed* young because of his nervousness, but he had to be in his late 30's. And I was 42 myself, so I wasn't usually up for delicate schoolgirl flirtations. As a rule, I was more direct. "Want to come over to my place and fuck?" But Alan seemed to demand a softer approach, and something about that intrigued me.

Later that day, I stopped off at the bathhouse on Toulouse Street in the Quarter, sucked two dicks and had my own dick sucked, and then I biked home to my house in the Marigny.

By the next day, I had completely forgotten about Alan.

I got down to my part-time job after lunch. I worked at home writing reviews for porno movies. I actually made about $400 a month doing this, but it was still only lagniappe. I couldn't have gotten by without my library job. I worked in the reference section on the main floor. Despite the internet, people still needed me occasionally.

I enjoyed reviewing porn, though. First of all, I enjoyed *watching* porn. And I enjoyed the fact that since I was a reviewer, I received the new porn DVDs for free. All I had to do was write my reaction to what I saw. I tried not to let my own specific interests make me too opinionated, but I found that I didn't have to say, "Oh, my god, how boring." I could just pretend to be objectively describing a scene but simply use boring words or exciting words to convey my opinion.

It was Thursday, but I had Thursdays off, and after watching two DVDs and beating off only at the end of the last one, I went downstairs to see if my mail had come.

I owned a two-story house in the Marigny that I had bought with my partner of twenty years, who had died almost three years ago of a heart attack at the age of 60. I lived on the top floor and rented out the downstairs as two small apartments. I had an entrance on the ground floor, naturally, and was walking down the stairs when I heard the metal squeak of the mail slot. Just in time, I thought.

But I stopped short when I realized there were eyes peering at me through the slot. I was only wearing my T-shirt and underwear, and I realized suddenly my underwear even had a little wet spot from where I'd leaked after coming.

Was that the mailman looking at me, I wondered. Well, whoever it was was going to get an eyeful.

I ran the rest of the way down the stairs and opened the door.

It was Alan, turning beet red.

"I—I was just—I mean—I—"

"What a perv," I said, laughing.

Alan turned even redder.

"You don't have to sneak a peek," I said, putting my hand on his shoulder. "I'll show you anything you want to see." I reached down to the elastic band on my boxer briefs.

"I've got to go." Alan turned and got on his bike and hurried off.

I laughed, but I couldn't help but think, "Hey, we've both got bikes. We'll have to go riding together sometime." I knew I'd have to stop by the bookstore again to tease him.

A few days later, I did stop in, and I was happy to see Alan at the register. "Hi, boyfriend," I said, smiling sweetly at him. He turned red. "Any new porn?"

"I don't know."

I left him alone then and browsed the card rack, looking for a racy birthday card to send to a friend. When I glanced back over at the counter, I could see Alan checking out my box.

He was almost squinting, of course, since I didn't have that showy a box, being more of a grower than a shower, but he was definitely trying hard to see what he could. I smiled, and he turned away quickly to do some paperwork.

I selected a card and went up to the counter. Alan didn't say anything, but when he handed me the card, I took his hand and held it, mostly just to see his reaction. I saw barely controlled panic in his eyes.

"What time is your shift over?"

"6:00. Why?"

"Have you ever seen *Under the Tuscan Sun*?"

"No. Why?"

"Do you like catfish?"

"Yes. Why?"

"You're coming over to my house when you get off work. We'll have a nice dinner and then watch a DVD."

Alan looked down at the counter. "I—I'm not really supposed to date," he said softly.

"You already have a boyfriend?" I asked. I think I let the surprise in my voice show.

"Oh, no. It's just that I'm Mormon. I'm supposed to be celibate. I've never gone on a date before."

"Well, I wasn't asking you to bed. Just to see a movie."

"Oh, I thought—I—"

"Not that I wouldn't have tried to make a move on you, but I can control myself, even around someone as good looking as you."

Alan turned red again.

"But we will have to cuddle while we watch. Will that work for you?"

"I—I suppose."

I didn't know why I was pursuing Alan so strongly. Part of it had to be just for the fun of watching him squirm. But I also did find him attractive, and while I had a good circle of friends already, I was always open to widening that circle. Gay people had to rely on chosen family more than biological family, and I always wanted more "relatives."

Alan and I did have dinner that evening, and we did cuddle while watching the movie. There was no fondling, though, and not even any kissing. I was touched at the end of the evening, however, when Alan stood up formally and offered me his hand. "I had a very good time," he said. "Thank you."

I grabbed his hand and pulled Alan close to me, kissing his ear. "Will you come back next Sunday?" I whispered.

"Y-yes," he whispered back.

Alan came over every Sunday evening for the next several weeks. His shift was only from noon to six, he explained, and he went to church with his mother every Sunday morning before work, and so, he went on, "I feel I just need to treat myself once a week." He looked guilty immediately and added, "You don't think that's a sin, do you? It's not like we're having sex or anything."

"Well, there *is* a little bit of 'anything,'" I said. "I do beat off thinking of you after you leave."

Alan turned red, but he smiled, too. "Really?" Then he looked concerned. "But if I make you sin, does that count as a sin against me, too?"

"I'm not sinning, honey."

Alan didn't say anything.

"If you think being gay is so bad, why do you work in a gay bookstore?"

"Well, I'm not sure anymore if it's bad. And I want to see a little of the other side of the question so I can make up my mind. I'd like not to be alone the rest of my life. I mean, I have my Mom, but…"

"I think you need to start coming over on Wednesday evenings, too."

"Really?" Alan smiled again.

"I have a lot of DVDs," I said. "Do you mind more cuddling?"

Alan thought for a moment. "I *like* cuddling," he said slowly.

"I get off work at 6:00 on Wednesdays. So can you be here at 7:00?"

We started doing other things besides watching movies. Sometimes, we played Scrabble or UNO or gin rummy and even games like Hangman and charades. I found Alan delightfully innocent and playful on the one hand, but on the other, I was a little disturbed to learn that at 38, he still lived at home with his Mom. She was in perfect health and didn't need a caretaker, but Alan felt that after his father's death fifteen years earlier, he had to look out for his mother. It seemed sweet in some ways, but in another way, I wondered if he hadn't really stayed 18 years old for the past 20 years.

Of course, *I* wasn't still just a kid, and while I was enjoying Alan's company, I was also actively pursuing the company of other men. Sometimes, I'd sit on the stoop in front of my front door and just pick up guys walking down the street. Other times late at night, I'd go to the bar three blocks away and pick someone up there.

I usually told Alan about these episodes. He looked perturbed but also always asked for details. Then he'd just look at the floor a moment and think.

One day, though, he surprised me by kissing me hello. "Wow," I said, "That's a big step."

Alan turned red but then looked a little depressed. "It's pretty sad when something as simple as a kiss is a big step."

"Well, let's be happy about it, not sad."

He looked up then and nodded. "Okay. I'm sorry. I guess I'm just in a down mood because I've decided maybe there is no God. I've been praying for something for a long time and God hasn't given it to me, so I finally realized maybe he doesn't exist."

"Hmm," I said, trying to keep this light. "Maybe he *does* exist, but he just doesn't like you." I smiled teasingly.

Alan's brow furrowed. "You know, with my low self-esteem, it's a wonder that never occurred to me."

"So you'll keep the faith a little longer?"

"Why do you want me to believe? I thought you disapproved of all my angst."

"Oh, there's nothing wrong with believing in God. It's just the believing that he doesn't want you to be loved by someone that I find upsetting."

Alan nodded. Of course, I hadn't myself prayed in a very long time, but I didn't see why Alan couldn't have both faith and love in his own life.

I decided to lighten things up now, though. I'd found an old game of Twister at a rummage sale, and after dinner, we improvised a way to play with just two people. When we were pretty entangled already, I then announced, "Left hand on right buttocks," and placed my hand on Alan's ass.

He jumped, but a moment later, I felt a hand on my ass as well.

He kissed me goodnight that evening as he left, and kissing became a regular part of our encounters from then on. I tried introducing it to the cuddling sessions, and after only a brief amount of resistance, Alan gave in and started some pretty good amateur French kissing. It didn't take him long to polish his technique, either.

He started staying longer after our Sunday night movie was over.

I found that Alan was truly a sweet man. He told me of his two years as a missionary in Tonga, where he helped teach people English as well as helped local Mormons build a couple of houses for some of the poorer islanders. I'd always thought Mormons just proselytized, so it was nice to hear they actually did some useful things, too.

And in the years since he returned to the States, Alan regularly volunteered with the Cub Scouts, and with the Sierra Club, and with an AIDS hospice, and with organizing local March of Dimes events.

"You think a lot about other people," I said.

"Well, to be honest, it's all just to divert the energy I *want* to put into sex. I sometimes wonder how many great things we could do as a people if we didn't invest so much of ourselves in seeking an orgasm."

"It doesn't have to be either/or," I said. "I teach ESL to Latino immigrants." I paused. "Of course, I make the men take their shirts off if they want any extra help."

"See what I mean?"

"You may have a point. But how about I make you a promise? After we start having sex, I'll begin volunteering with the Sierra Club, too."

Alan turned red, but he looked pensive for a few moments as well.

But we didn't start having sex. Soon, we'd been "dating" for five months, and I had yet to so much as grope him. He did let me rub his chest during our cuddling sessions, and he would rub mine, too, but if my hand strayed down to his stomach, he would grasp it and place it back on his chest.

We did a few day excursions, too, biking together through the Marigny or to Audubon Park, buying fruit at the Farmers Market, walking slowly along the levee, and even going to gay bingo once. I found Alan intelligent, and we talked about the Middle East, and about health care reform, and about nuclear and solar and wind energy, and even about astronomy. Sometimes, we watched lectures on DVD about topics like Greek archaeology or Jewish intellectual thought of the 16th century.

"You know," I told him one day over gumbo, "if I could just get you into bed, you'd make a great husband."

"There's so much else we can share," Alan replied. "Shouldn't that be enough?"

"But when you love someone, you want to share yourself with them completely."

"I love my mother, but I don't want to have sex with her. And what relationship can be stronger than that between a mother and son?"

"That between a married couple."

Alan looked at the floor a moment. "Maybe," he said slowly. "Maybe."

It was on our six-month "anniversary" that I was finally able to meet Alan's mother, in their Gentilly home. She hadn't heard anything about me, I learned, and thought I was a regular at the straight French Quarter bookstore where Alan worked. He'd told her months ago that he also worked at a gay bookstore, and they'd talked a few times about his feelings toward men in general, but she was only okay about his "being" gay, he told me, as long as he wasn't "doing" gay things.

"Like listening to old disco songs?" I asked him.

Alan glared at me but laughed.

"So you're a friend of Alan's?" his mother asked me that evening, shaking my hand as she let me into her home. "I'm Sharon."

"I'm Balzer," I said.

"What an odd name." She smiled.

"It suits me," I replied. "Because I'm ballsy."

"Oh, dear. We try not to use language like that around here. I hope I'm not offending you."

"Oh, no. I'm a librarian. I'm used to attempts at censorship." I smiled, and she smiled back uncertainly.

But after our rocky start, I found I really liked Alan's mother. She was a social worker who also volunteered with the Breast Cancer Run and the Brownies. As an active Mormon, she naturally taught Sunday school every week, but she also made a point of being pen pals with three children in South America she was sending money to every month, teaching herself Spanish on the side. I suppose after fifteen years without a husband, she was deflecting some sexual energy, too. Still, there were plenty of more selfish ways to do that. She seemed like a legitimately nice woman to me.

"I don't know if Alan has told you," Sharon said, "but we only just got our stove working again. We had to cook on the grill for a whole week." She shook her head. "I tried hard to be creative…"

"But it's just so difficult to grill those peas," I continued for her.

Sharon laughed, a hearty, sweet, good-natured laugh. "It was the red beans and rice that was the toughest."

"She's not kidding," said Alan.

We had a pleasant, cheerful meal, and I could see why Alan genuinely liked his mother, though I was still a little concerned that she had too much control over her son's life.

"Now tell me," Sharon said over dessert a little later. "Alan's been very secretive. But he stays out late a couple of times a week. Do you think he's got a sweetheart? Does he talk to you about these things?"

"He's been very vague," I replied, "but I think he may be seeing someone special."

"Oh, I hope so." She paused a moment. "Are you married, Balzer?"

"I was married for twenty years. But three years ago after a terrible heart attack…"

"Oh, and so young. How awful."

"Yes, it was awful. I'm sure your loss was awful for you, too."

"Yes." She nodded slowly. "But you find ways of coping." She smiled at Alan.

"I had a friend," I said suddenly, "a woman named Ann. She had a sister, but her sister left home at 20. That left Ann alone with her parents, who hadn't gotten married till they were over 40. So they were in their 60's by then. Ann felt she had to stay home and take care of them. Of course, they lived until their mid-80's. By the time Ann allowed herself to date, she was 45 herself. She did finally marry at 48, but naturally, she'll never have children. She felt she was doing a good thing by staying with her parents, but she gave up her whole life to do it."

"Greater love hath no man than this, that a man give up his life for a friend," said Sharon, apparently quoting some scripture.

"Then why shouldn't it be the parent giving up *their* 'life' for their child?" I asked.

There was silence for a moment. Then Sharon said slowly, "Do you have any children?"

"No."

"I didn't think so."

"I think your friend Ann stayed with her parents because she *wanted* to," said Alan, "not because she *had* to. There's a difference."

Sharon smiled again.

The dinner was over by then, and I only stayed about fifteen more minutes, as I could clearly see Sharon had had enough of me for one evening. But she smiled sweetly and shook my hand at the door as I left. I couldn't read Alan's expression as he said goodbye.

Alan didn't call the next day, or the next, but he did show up again on Wednesday night. He kissed me and hugged me when he came in the door.

"Oh, what a scene you caused," he said, plopping down on the sofa. "My mother cried for half an hour, asking if she was ruining my life. It took me forever to convince her that I liked things just the way they are."

"Why would you want to convince her of that?"

"Because she was crying."

"So if I start crying, you'll begin sleeping over?"

Alan looked at me.

"I took acting in college. I can be very convincing."

"My mother isn't acting."

"I think you stay with your mother because you're comfortable there. She does the cooking and the cleaning, and you don't have to face any adult responsibilities."

"Always being there for someone is an adult responsibility."

"What are you going to do when you're 55 or 60 and your mother dies? You'll be all alone in the world."

"She'll be all alone *now* if I leave her."

"I think most men with wives and children still manage to call their mothers and visit. And there's no reason she can't try to make a few friends and stop forcing you to be her only social support. Aren't there any nice people at your church?"

Alan was quiet a moment.

"I want you to start sleeping over one night a week."

"I don't want to have sex."

"I didn't say anything about sex. I just want to feel you beside me all night. Your mother still has you six nights a week. I'm not asking for the world. But I need you over here at least one night a week."

Alan looked at the floor. "What will I tell my mother?"

"Tell her anything you want."

"She'll think I'm having sex if I stay out all night. I couldn't do it."

I was quite irritated by this point and wanted to say, "Are you wearing diapers? Be a man!" but instead I said, "Can't you just sneak over and then sneak back home early in the morning?"

Alan continued looking at the floor. "Maybe," he said slowly. "Maybe."

Two weeks later, on a Wednesday night, Alan stayed for his first sleepover, or as we decided to call it, his "sneakover." We had our usual evening together first, then Alan rode his bike back home, made a show of going to bed, and then sneaked back over after his mother fell asleep. We debated about whether to have the sneakover at his place or mine and finally decided that it wouldn't feel like a grown up thing to do unless we did it at my place.

As we were cuddling with the lights out, still wearing our underwear (and Alan's Mormon underwear certainly took some getting used to), I said, "I'm going to tell you a bedtime story."

"Okay," said Alan, giggling, and holding my arm tightly across his chest.

I then proceeded to outline a scenario from one of the porn DVDs I'd had to review the night before. I was determined not to let this evening be just the equivalent of a preteen slumber party.

"Oh, you're mean," said Alan, but he laughed anyway.

He could feel my dick growing hard against his backside and he pressed his ass up against me, but there was no official fondling. Still, I thought it was a step forward for us, and I fell asleep pretty contentedly.

I wondered over the following weeks if all this effort was worth it. Alan was clearly damaged goods and would never be "normal." Of course, who in this life wasn't noticeably damaged in some way? But even if we did start having sex, there was no guarantee we'd be compatible in the first place. Besides, there would be so much pressure to perform well after all this foreplay that it was bound to be a little disappointing, even if it was actually quite adequate.

But I liked the guy. Even if Alan were no good in bed, I could still get my rocks off with other men, as I was doing now. I just wanted to be with him. As irritated as I was with Sharon, I had to admit she'd raised a good son.

One Sunday when Alan showed up, I said, "Want to help me with some work?"

"What do you need?"

"I've got another DVD I have to review."

"I don't know," Alan said cautiously. "I've never watched porn before. I've heard it's addictive."

"Well, I have an endless supply. You'll never have to go through withdrawal."

"I don't know."

"If you get too excited, you can go in the bathroom and beat off by yourself. I won't take advantage of you."

Alan looked a little dejected at that, it seemed, which made me smile. "If you want to understand the gay world, or be comfortable in that world, you have to at least be exposed to a little porn."

Alan looked at the floor. "Okay," he said softly.

He giggled during the first ten minutes of the movie, but then his brows furrowed as he began to concentrate. We didn't talk the whole time. I was taking notes and didn't pause the action as I might normally have done. I wasn't sure Alan would be able to take an entire DVD, but he sat on the sofa next to me till the very end. Then, without a word, he went to the bathroom. I smiled.

I felt a brief flash of guilt, though, wondering if I was corrupting a pure man. But I believed in God, too, and I believed God gave us sex to help make our lives better. What was corrupt was making people feel like dirt when they were sharing one of the few real pleasures in a usually difficult life.

Alan had told me a little about his theology, how sex was reserved in the hereafter only for those people who'd lived the best lives and were the most righteous. When Alan came out of the bathroom now, he looked a little worried, so I said, "If it's okay for the righteous to enjoy their bodies for eternity," I said, "why is it a mortal sin to do it now?"

"Because we *are* mortal. The rules are different here."

"Money can be used selfishly, to buy a hundred pairs of shoes, or to feed the hungry," I said. "Books can be used to elevate the mind, like *To Kill a Mockingbird*, or they can be like *Mein Kampf* and used to hurt people. Sex can be used to degrade people or exercise power and control, or it can be used to make people feel good and loved. Anything can be used positively or negatively. But just because something *can* be used negatively doesn't mean the thing itself is necessarily always bad. Don't throw the baby out with the bathwater."

Alan looked at the floor, his brows furrowed. "Maybe," he said.

"How do you feel right now?"

"I don't know. I've fantasized about some of those things before, so I don't know that it's any worse to actually watch it." He paused. "It was oddly satisfying, and yet…"

"And yet…"

"Somehow it made me think that just getting off vicariously would somehow be a lesser thing than real sex."

"Duh."

"That it would be a Telestial act rather than a Celestial one."

"You're getting too Mormon on me."

"The bottom line is that it makes masturbation not seem as satisfying as it used to be."

"Oh, don't give up jacking off. Even after you start having sex with others, it's still fun to have sex with yourself. There's no sin in loving yourself, too."

Alan looked at the floor. "I wonder."

But I felt we'd made a breakthrough, and every Sunday night thereafter, I asked Alan to "help" me with my reviews. It felt like the world's longest seduction, but we were both enjoying every minute of the attempt. Alan was perfectly aware of what I was doing, but he seemed quite willing to let me pull him slowly along.

I thought things were going pretty well, but one Thursday evening, Alan knocked on my door, on an unscheduled visit. "My Mom almost caught me coming in this morning. I just don't know if I can sleep over any more. It would be too awful if she found out."

"Alan," I said calmly. "What's the worst she can do if she finds out you're sleeping over here?"

"She might say something about me being 'confused' rather than gay."

"So she makes some remarks. That's it?"

"Well, she also might just ignore it and keep it to herself."

"Great. Then she shuts up and minds her own business."

"Well..."

"None of that sounds all that terrible to me. It's not like she can disown you and move to Acapulco."

"There's another possibility."

"What's that?"

"She might feel sad."

That one threw me for a second. Then I said slowly, "Well, *I'll* feel sad if you don't sleep over. And *you'll* feel sad, too. That makes it two to one. Is it right for her to make us sad?"

"I'm not sure that's fair," said Alan. "If it makes 40 million Germans happy to make 6 million Jews unhappy, do the numbers make it right?"

That threw me a little, too. "I just think at some point we have an obligation to live our own life. It's an absolute obligation. God gave you life, and it's not yours to throw away. You have to live while you're alive."

"Well, it's not like my life is meaningless now. I have a good job. I earn my way in the world. I read interesting books. I do good things for people. I have a good friend I really care about. That's not nothing, is it?"

I waited a moment before speaking. "I value your friendship. But I've had a partner before. And I know from experience that loving someone so much they're you're best friend *and* your lover is better than having someone who is just a friend. There's certainly a place for platonic friendship, but there's a place for sexual love, too. Adam and Eve had that. The prophet in your church has it. It's not something to toss aside like so much garbage."

"Gandhi was celibate the last couple of decades of his life."

"Are your apostles abstinent? Does your church teach that abstinence is a higher way?"

"Only for gays."

"You said that even God has sex with his wives in heaven. Are you higher than God?"

"If there is a God," Alan mumbled. "Why would a god feel the need to torture me all my life?"

"This is crippling your chance at happiness, with me or anyone else. Are you sure you're not just using your mother as a gatekeeper or a scarecrow? I think maybe you're just avoiding taking responsibility for your own ambivalence about intimacy."

"I've been trying."

"Fifteen-year-old boys try harder than you. You're an adult. You can't stay a shy teenager your whole life."

Alan started crying, and though I was irritated with him, I moved over and hugged him.

"Please help me," he said, still sniffling. "Please love me enough to put up with me."

We lay down on the bed for a few moments so I could hold him close against me.

I decided to try a new approach after this. I'd been keeping Alan to myself, a little selfishly perhaps, but I thought maybe exposing him now to other gay men might help him feel more comfortable about "our world." I hoped working in the gay bookstore was helping, too. He'd gotten some propositions there, but he hadn't made any friends among the regulars. I wanted Alan to have a larger network of gay men in his life.

On Tuesday night, I usually played cards with a few friends, so I asked if I could bring Alan along, and they were all anxious to meet "the Mormon." We simply chatted as we played, saying nothing particularly deep or meaningful.

"I'm going on a cruise this summer," said Ted, one of the group. "But I'm telling everyone I meet there that I'm 55 instead of 40. They'll all be saying how good I look."

"My last vacation was back in 1995," said David, another card player. "I mean, 2005," he corrected himself. "I hate when I get the wrong time, I mean, the wrong period, I mean, the wrong decade."

"The wrong lifetime?" I suggested.

"Yes, that's so annoying."

"Well, I have the right lifetime," said Peter, the last in our group. "Jared and I just celebrated our seventh anniversary."

"How's the itch?" asked Ted.

"You have to be careful when you say that to a gay man," countered David. "That could mean so many different things in our community."

"I bought Jared an expensive new shirt for our anniversary. He likes to look good. In fact, this is one of his shirts I've got on now."

"You wear his clothes?"

"All the time. I hate to do laundry, and he insists on doing his own clothes. So I wear his things, and he has to clean them."

We all laughed.

"He complains and asks why I always wear his clothes."

"'So I can feel closer to you,'" suggested Alan.

We all laughed again.

"Good answer," said Peter. "You have the makings of an annoying lover."

The evening continued in much the same way, with meaningless banter over a meaningless card game. Alan seemed to enjoy himself, and I asked the others later if it would be okay to add him to our Tuesday nights. They all consented, and soon, Alan and I were seeing each other three nights a week.

The sneakovers continued unabated, even after Sharon discovered one night that Alan was gone. She went into a fit the next day, claiming she thought Alan had been murdered and she was up the rest of the night worrying.

"But she didn't call the police, did she?" I asked. "Or call the hospitals? She didn't ask for a name, did she? She's not stupid. She knew where you were."

I was impressed that Alan managed to avoid explaining where he was on his nights out, and managed to keep coming despite his mother's displeasure with it.

But a few weeks later, Alan stopped by with some bad news.

"My Mom has a lump in her breast," he said gloomily. "She goes in for a biopsy in a couple of days, and it'll be another week or so before she gets the results. I need to be at home with her."

"She'll be okay," I said softly. "Even if it's cancer, they'll get it in time."

"You understand why I can't stay, don't you?"

"Sure. I understand."

I did understand, but I was still irritated, though I felt like a heel because of my reaction. Obviously, Sharon couldn't have implanted the lump just to obstruct us, but it somehow still seemed calculating. Was there even a lump at all, I wondered? Or was all this just a ruse to get her boy back?

I had wondered if Sharon might start having dizzy spells or some other minor problem if she ever discovered Alan was sleeping over, but breast cancer was another thing. If it turned out to be serious, Alan would be gone for months. While I did truly love him, I realized suddenly, I wasn't sure I was up to waiting for him.

"Do you love me?" I asked.

"What?"

"Will you come back to me later, no matter how things turn out with your mother?"

"Yes," said Alan. "I promise I'll be back."

Either I called Alan or he called me every night over the next several days, but we only talked a few minutes before I could hear Sharon calling out for him in the background.

But as it happened, my own life got busier because my friend David from cards was starting work on a calendar that was going to be used as a fundraiser for some local HIV charities. He was a photographer and wanted to take photos of naked men.

"Charity work can be so trying," I said.

But I decided to get involved, and over the next couple of weeks, David set up three photo shoots. The first model shoot was in the hot tub at David's house. I got to apply the foam in the shoot.

David also had a private and jungly backyard, so he decided to use that as a setting for his second shoot with a handsome math instructor from Loyola. I got to apply the baby oil this time.

The third photo shoot took place in an out-of-the-way voodoo temple in Bywater, just down the river a few blocks from the Marigny. It turned out the temple priest was good looking enough to be right for the photos, so I was happy to attend this session as well, and got to light the candles.

What with card night and the library and the porn DVDs and the photo shoots and my occasional forays to the baths and to the bars, I realized I could still lead a perfectly happy life without Alan, if it turned out he saw the cancer as divine retribution and slowly faded out of my life.

I still *wanted* Alan, though, and I was pleasantly surprised when he showed up at my door one Monday evening a couple of days later.

"How's your mom?" I asked.

"She's fine. The lump wasn't cancerous."

I pulled Alan inside and gave him a hug and started kissing him. He kissed back enthusiastically.

"You need any help with your reviews tonight?" He smiled.

"Sure." I waved for him to follow.

We went upstairs and kicked off our shoes, falling down together on the sofa. "So what have you been up to?" Alan asked eagerly.

I took Alan's feet in my lap and started rubbing them while I told him in detail about the photo shoots. When I finished, he pulled his feet away and sat up stiffly.

"I don't want you doing things like that anymore," he said. "You're *my* boyfriend."

I looked at him with what I hoped was tenderness and said, "I'm not a priest, you know."

"I am," Alan said sadly. "Since I was 16."

"You could come along on some of the photo shoots if you like. I'm sure David would be okay with that."

Alan stared at the floor. "I can't keep living my life by proxy." He laughed rather bitterly and shook his head. "You know, in our temples, we do baptisms for the dead by proxy, and marriages by proxy. I don't want to live my whole life as if I'm not really here in person."

"So what are you going to do about it?"

"I think we're going to skip the porn tonight."

He pulled me close and kissed me slowly. Then he took my hand and placed it on his crotch. I squeezed softly, and he moaned. We pulled away for a moment and looked in each other's eyes. Then he nodded gently and pulled me close again.

Two and a half hours later, Alan rested his head on my arm as we lay in bed. He held my other arm against his chest. It was the first time I'd felt the hair on his chest without the buffer of his Mormon underwear.

"I hope you understand that I'm going to be insatiable for a while," he said.

"I'll make the sacrifice," I replied. "For your sake."

Alan laughed. There was a lightness to it this time.

We lay there quietly after that and slowly fell asleep in each other's arms.

I was anxious to see Alan's reaction in the morning, though, when he'd realize more fully what had happened, but he was smiling as we ate a bowl of cereal, our first breakfast together ever, since he hadn't felt the need to sneak back home at the crack of dawn today.

"My mother may have been the reigning queen all these years," said Alan, "but I'm not going to be the prince-in-waiting anymore."

"No, you're officially a queen now, too."

We laughed.

I got ready for work, and we went downstairs together to leave. "I'll see you for cards tonight," I said, kissing Alan as I locked the door behind us. We both climbed on our bicycles but gave each other one last long look before getting ready to take off in different directions.

"I learned something last night," said Alan.

"What's that?"

"There definitely is a God," he said. "And he does love me."

"He's not the only one." I paused and then grinned. "The Sierra Club loves you, too. I keep my promises."

Alan smiled, blew me a kiss, and started pedaling off. I smiled, too. 42 and 38 suddenly seemed very young to me.

I made my way through the Quarter, heading Uptown, and watched people hosing down the sidewalks as I passed.

I had a lover now. It *was* better than just having a good friend. It *was* better to have both, and to love the man you were having sex with.

I waved at the men cleaning the rubber floor mats outside the bars and kept going, still smiling. I was going to have a good day.

And I was going to see Alan again tonight.

I started whistling an old disco tune and then, giggling happily, offered up a prayer of thanksgiving into the early morning sky.

The Hotel Room

"Well, Houston, you're definitely expanding my horizons," said Sefton after a brief moment of silence.

"How does it feel?" I asked. I hoped I could show him that everybody had options, and it was more satisfying to live life out in the open. He was clearly going to realize by this point that I had lived in both New Orleans and Seattle, but it wasn't as if I was keeping back any other important personal information. While I was getting him to open up to me, I felt some unexplainable need to open up to him as well.

"Better than I thought." Sefton looked pensive, and I wondered if I should interrupt his thoughts. I wanted him to understand that the gay world had room for everyone, even fucked up Mormons. I really wasn't sure if I was even aware myself of all the messages I was sending his way tonight. My subconscious was probably hard at work trying to teach both of us things we needed to learn. Just as I was about to speak, Sefton continued, "What do you think about porn?"

I laughed. "What a question." Had talking about the reviewer turned him on? I'd told so many different kinds of stories for just that reason—to awaken him to every possibility. "It's great. Why?"

Sefton sighed. "I've never looked at porn."

My eyes must have widened because Sefton looked embarrassed and turned away. "Never?" I asked.

He shook his head.

"No magazines?"

"No."

"No movies?"

"No."

"No *internet*?"

He shook his head vigorously. "That kind of stuff can be traced, you know."

I nodded. "But you can't really mean *never*, can you? You just mean *not much*."

"I mean never. I'm afraid it'll be addictive, just like Alan said."

"Sefton," I said carefully, "pornography isn't magic. It isn't going to cast a spell on you. If you're not interested, don't look. I have gay friends who don't look very often. It just doesn't appeal to them. But for heaven's sake, you're not going to be struck by lightning for looking."

"It *is* for heaven's sake that I don't look."

I fluffed my pillow and leaned back against the headboard. "Are there any actresses you find beautiful?" I asked.

Sefton frowned. "Sure. Sandra Bullock is pretty. And Eliza Dushku. And from old shows, I thought Elizabeth Montgomery and Stephanie Zimbalist were beautiful."

"If you're not attracted to women, how can you find them beautiful?"

Sefton shrugged. "I often wondered that myself. It gave me hope. Then I finally realized I must just appreciate them the way I'd appreciate a work of art or a scenic countryside."

"You can approach porn the same way," I said, "just enjoy looking at beautiful men because they're beautiful."

"But porn…"

"Gets you excited. So what's the difference between fantasizing about a man and actually seeing one? Why is one worse than the other, if they're both just to get you off?"

Sefton was silent a long moment. "I don't know," he finally said.

"I'm not going to say you *have* to look, only that you shouldn't be afraid all the time about everything."

He sighed again. "It's tiring to be afraid all the time," he admitted.

I pointed to the remote on the bedside table. "There's a DVD player here," I said, "and I brought a nice DVD in my bag tonight." Having the machine was a bit of luck. Lots of hotels didn't offer them.

"Such a Boy Scout," he said with a sad smile.

I went to my bag and rummaged inside it. "Eagle," I confirmed.

"I'm afraid."

"I'm not going to push," I said, "but do you want me to put it in so that we can watch just for five minutes?"

Sefton didn't say anything, so after a minute, I turned on the television, slid in the DVD, and soon found enticing images on the screen. Sefton kept his eyes averted to begin with, but after my first "Ooh! Nice abs!" he turned to look. We watched for fifteen minutes, and I not only enjoyed the movie but also the break it gave me from storytelling. At first, Sefton stood near the window, watching from a great distance, holding his shirt in front of him as if he planned to put it on, but little by little he drew closer to the bed, and he finally tossed his shirt back onto a chair. After seeing several wonderfully graphic sex acts, he could no longer control himself, and he started fondling me again. I rarely came more than twice in one evening, but soon we were fully engaged for a third time. And it was just as enthralling this go around as it had been the previous two times.

Thirty minutes later, Sefton lay back with his hands behind his head. "I feel like I just drank a fully caffeinated Coke," he said. "This has been the greatest night of my life."

I laughed. "It's not over yet," I said. "You up for another story?" I thought I'd tell him one to really force my point, and I knew, one way or the other, it would be the last tale of the evening.

"You're bound and determined, aren't you?" He laughed.

"Perseverance has always been one of my strong points."

"Well, it's a good character trait. I admire it." He motioned to me graciously. "Go ahead, sweetie. I'm all ears."

The Mission

Elder Whyte looked at the line of first-graders crossing the street. He and Elder King lived just a block from an elementary school in their missionary district in the northern part of Kansas City. That was Kansas City, Missouri. Elder Whyte couldn't believe he'd been lucky enough to be assigned to work in Jackson County, where the Garden of Eden had once been, and where Jesus would be coming back to inaugurate the Millennium.

"It must be great to work with kids," Elder Whyte said to the crossing guard, who had moved back to the curb to wait for the next group of children to gather.

"They're little monsters," the man muttered. "I ought to let them get run over."

Elder King laughed, and the crossing guard did, too. Elder Whyte didn't laugh, though. That didn't seem particularly funny to him.

Elder Whyte looked at the two young children who'd just walked up to the corner. So innocent and lovely. He'd been about that age, he remembered now, when he asked his father, "Where did I come from?" His father had sighed and then gone into a horrifying explanation of sex. When he was finished, his father asked, "Does that answer your question?" Elder Whyte, six years old at the time, had answered doubtfully, "Well, we live in Philadelphia, and I thought I came from Pittsburg." His father had laughed and laughed, but Elder Whyte was still too upset by the discussion to see any humor in the incident, then or now.

"Come on, Elder Whyte," said King suddenly. "There's the bus. We can catch it if we run."

The two missionaries ran half a block, but the driver closed the door in their faces and pulled off. Anti-Mormon, clearly.

But it wasn't the first discrimination Elder Whyte had faced here on his mission. He'd been out almost a year, and he'd been spit on three times, been cursed out more times than he could remember, and awakened one morning to find a swastika painted on his door. Why anyone would compare Mormons to Nazis, he didn't know.

Elder Whyte and Elder King talked for a few minutes about their upcoming Preparation Day tomorrow, during which they planned to go to the park and play two-man soccer. Elder Whyte was hoping that it would be a special day. They worked six days a week. He tried to make every P-Day memorable. It wasn't that the missionary work wasn't phenomenal, he told himself. It was just that even God needed rest from righteous labor, and Elder Whyte did, too.

"You guys play soccer?" asked a man perhaps a few years older than they were, in his early twenties, who'd just walked up to the bus stop and who was now standing beside them. He'd clearly overheard their discussion.

"Oh, it's just the two of us," said Elder King, "but we like to kick the ball around."

"Can I join you sometime? I like to get my exercise, too."

The man looked wonderfully fit, thought Elder Whyte. He hoped the man would play with his shirt off. Then he bit the inside of his cheek to punish himself for his sinful thoughts. It was such a burden, he realized again, to spend your whole life knowing you were going to hell. Most people didn't know till their test of Earth life was over, but he had 70 more years to live, knowing the final test results ahead of time.

"We're playing tomorrow around noon in the park," said King. "Is that good for you?"

"If you make it 1:00, I can come on my lunch hour. Would that work for you guys?"

"Sure. 1:00 is fine. We'll meet you by the fruit tree in front of the park."

"Sounds great. I'm Stan, by the way." He offered his hand.

"I'm Elder King."

"Elder Whyte."

"Elder?"

"We're missionaries for the Church of Jesus Christ of Latter-day Saints."

"I'm agnostic."

"We can work on that." Elder King smiled, and Stan did, too. It was a nice smile, Elder Whyte thought.

Soon the bus came, and they all climbed on. Stan got off about a mile away, but Elders Whyte and King stayed on a while longer. They had a member family to visit this morning. They visited several member families each week, for the purpose of strengthening the locals in their commitment to the gospel, but also in the hopes of getting some good referrals. They rarely got any names and addresses of interested people, but it was pleasant work visiting the members.

The Johnson family they were visiting today was a mom and two young children. An older child was in elementary school. The husband, of course, was at work. Elder Whyte felt that having the children interact regularly with the missionaries would make it more likely the kids would grow up to serve the Church, too.

"Elders!" said Sister Johnson as she opened the door. "It's always great to see you. Come on in."

"Elder Whyte!" squealed a little three-year-old boy. He ran to Elder Whyte and hugged his leg.

"Peter! How you doing today?"

Elder Whyte picked up the boy and gave him a hug. A lot of kids these days didn't like hugs, but Peter always hugged Elder Whyte tightly, and it made Elder Whyte feel good. He wasn't sure he'd ever manage to get married and have children of his own, but he wanted to be around that purity as much as possible, and he'd work to keep his own children innocent until they were adults, if he ever did have any.

At least he'd keep them innocent till they were well past the age of eight. It always seemed such a shame to Elder Whyte that parents let their children grow up so fast. By the time they reached the age of accountability and were baptized, they must have switched over immediately to Telestial Kingdom status. Parents needed to keep their children worthy of the Celestial Kingdom even after they turned eight. People were supposed to improve with every birthday, not get worse, but there were too many things in the world which destroyed innocence.

"Elder King, you have a little bit of a cough there. You're not going to give it to my kids, are you?" Sister Johnson laughed, but she looked a little concerned as well.

"It just started this morning. Maybe we better not stay long."

"I lost my second-born when he was just a little older than Peter is now. That's why there's such a gap between the oldest and these two."

"Oh, I'm sorry. I didn't know."

"It was hard, but being in the Church helped me through it. And it gives me the commitment to live right so I'll see her again in the Celestial Kingdom." She laughed brightly. "God only knows if Richard, my oldest, will make it. He gets in trouble at school all the time."

"All we can do is guide them," said Elder Whyte, "and hope they follow our example." It didn't quite seem like enough. He knew he was sinning by thinking so, but sometimes he felt as if he understood Satan's rejected plan to come down and force people to be good. You couldn't really count on people to do it themselves. Here Elder Whyte was, born into a third-generation LDS family, raised right, with two older brothers and a father who'd served missions, his father on the stake high council now, and Elder Whyte was still destined for hell because of his wickedness. He often prayed to Heavenly Father to make him straight, but God wouldn't do it, and if God was going to leave it up to Elder Whyte to be good, it didn't seem as if it was ever going to happen.

They visited with Sister Johnson for just fifteen minutes and then went out to do some tracting. After an unsuccessful hour of that, Elder Whyte suggested distributing his flyers. It wasn't a mission program, but he'd developed the idea on his own, to make up flyers inviting families to send their early teen boys to the Boy Scout troop of the local LDS congregation, and inviting the older teen boys to play on the ward basketball team, and the girls to play volleyball. Elder Whyte paid for the flyers with his own money, skimping on a couple of meals each week. But he felt that getting people involved in Church activities, even if they weren't initially interested in the lessons, would all eventually lead to something good. You had to get people while they were still young.

Of course, he and his companion had been putting out flyers a couple of times a week for two months now, and they had yet to see anyone show up at an activity. But you couldn't simply give up, could you? You had to try to find a way to capture the youth before they became too deeply caught up in the ways of the world.

It finally became tedious not to be talking to anyone, however, so the missionaries started tracting again. No one seemed interested, though, as usual. Just how, Elder Whyte wondered, could he bring any souls to God, if no one would listen?

"Mormons, huh?" said one woman who answered her door. "I saw you on the news last night. One of your prophets was arrested in Nevada for marrying a 15-year-old girl and her 14-year-old sister."

"Mormons don't practice polygamy," Elder King said, but the woman gave a condescending nod and closed her door firmly.

"I hate that people still believe we practice polygamy," said Elder King as they walked away.

"Well, we do, don't we?" asked Elder Whyte. "My uncle was married to my aunt in the temple, and when she died, he married another woman in the temple. We believe in polygamy in the afterlife."

The idea worried him. He wondered if somehow he did make it to the Celestial Kingdom despite being gay, if he'd have to marry more than one woman there. What must it have been like for the early Mormons who were gay and told they had to have several wives? Elder Whyte couldn't imagine how awful it must have been to have sex regularly with five different women when he didn't even want to do it with one.

"That's not the same thing," said Elder King. "I'm from Salt Lake, and no one does it there."

Elder Whyte let it drop, but when they went home for lunch later, Elder King brought up the subject of sex yet again. "My girlfriend and I have talked about what kinds of things we want to do sexually once we get married," he said as the two young men munched on sandwiches. "Do you and your girlfriend ever talk about it?"

Elder Whyte had never had a girlfriend. He'd told people he didn't want to date before his mission because he didn't want to punish a girl by making her wait two years for him to return, and he didn't want to be distracted from the Lord's work. So while the other priests in his ward started dating at 16, Elder Whyte had just focused on school and his seminary studies.

Everyone seemed to believe him, though, and thought he was super-righteous. It made him feel like a jerk, knowing the real reason was because he was super-sinful.

"Don't you find that talking about it creates too much temptation?" asked Elder Whyte.

"No," said King. "It helps defuse the tension instead." He paused and then added, "You want to hear the kinds of things we plan to do?"

Elder Whyte tried not to look shocked but quickly shook his head. Why did Elder King need to talk about such things now? Did he need to "defuse" some of his sexual tension today? Why was he feeling so much sexual tension right now anyway? Elder Whyte felt it all the time, of course, but that was because gays had such carnal natures to begin with.

Elder King shrugged, and they ate the rest of their meal in silence, except for Elder King's occasional coughing. Elder Whyte noticed, though, that Elder King took a long time in the bathroom before they went out again later. Whyte realized that King might just be defecating, but he couldn't help but suspect that maybe King was masturbating instead. That was strictly forbidden, of course, not just for missionaries but for any unwed members. Whyte understood that the reason he succumbed to this temptation himself almost weekly was because of his natural depravity. But he couldn't help but wonder if some of the straight missionaries felt tempted at times, too. He imagined King in the bathroom now with his hands on his body and he felt himself growing hard. He pinched his arm till it bruised and reached over to open his scriptures.

They did a little more tracting in the afternoon, and a Catholic woman let them in for a bit. Her cousin's baby had just died moments after birth, about two weeks previously, and the family had not had time to baptize the infant before she died. "Will she go to Limbo?" asked the woman nervously. "We've all been so worried about it, and our priest says the baby simply can't go to Heaven without baptism. What do you folks believe?"

"We believe that baptism is necessary, too," began Elder King, but after seeing the woman's expression, he quickly added, "but we do baptisms on behalf of the dead in our temples, by proxy for those who died without a chance to be baptized. So there's no need to worry."

"We believe all children under eight go straight to God's presence when they die," added Elder Whyte. "How can an hour-old baby have committed any sins?"

"Well, there's always original sin…" the woman began hesitantly.

"But how can an infant be responsible for something someone else did? God is fair, not mean."

The woman was intrigued enough to let them teach the first lesson, but she grew less open when the two missionaries discussed Joseph Smith's first vision as a 14-year-old boy. She thanked them politely after they were finished and showed them to the door.

Walking back to the bus stop, Elder Whyte thought about what he'd said to the woman. If an infant wasn't responsible for Adam and Eve's sin, why was Elder Whyte responsible for being gay, something he didn't choose? It was a condition forced on him by nature or DNA or something outside of himself. He remembered his mother laughing as she recalled a time when Whyte was just five, and she'd announced at the dinner table that it was movie night, and they were all going to sit down as a family after they finished eating and watch a movie. Elder Whyte had replied, "I hope there's a prettier man in it this week." The week before, they'd watched an old John Wayne movie, and Elder Whyte had not been impressed with his beauty. He must have been gay even then.

But if he'd died at age five, he'd still have gone to the Celestial Kingdom. Yet now he was an abomination.

Elder King pulled a cord, and the two got off at the Safeway to pick up a few things. The next day was Elder Whyte's twentieth birthday, and though he hadn't told King about it, he did still want to get a cheap cake. They were really only supposed to shop on P-Day, but they actually did it whenever they felt like it. Whyte was afraid of committing any extra sins, but he agreed today because he did want that cake. Birthdays always made him feel like a kid again, and he liked that feeling.

They grabbed a cart and put in some bread and cold cuts and a few frozen dinners and some apples. But then Elder King pointed to a man putting fresh produce in his basket. Elder Whyte had noticed him, too. He was a good looking man. "Let's go get him," his companion said.

"How do you cook that zucchini?" Elder King asked the man, smiling in a friendly manner. "I tried it once, and it got all soggy."

The man looked at Elder King and then at Elder Whyte, and then he moved on without a word. But Elder King wasn't giving up, Whyte realized. He followed the man and asked, "What do you know about the Mormon Church?" The man continued on, still without speaking, and Elder King added, "Would you like to know more?"

At this point, the man stopped a produce clerk and said, "These two guys are harassing me. You need to kick them out of the store."

The clerk looked over, and his eyes rested briefly on Elder Whyte's nametag. Then he hooked his thumb in the direction of the door, and King and Whyte left their cart and walked away.

"Persecuted for the sake of the gospel," said Elder King as they made their way back to the bus stop. "I hope we get points for that."

"We need to stop at another grocery," said Whyte.

"There's no more time today. We'll stop by someplace tomorrow." He went into a long coughing spasm for a couple of minutes. "I'm not feeling very well, anyway. Maybe we better just stop by to see the Fallises and then call it a night."

They had a dinner appointment once or twice a week with different members of the congregation, and tonight they were scheduled to see the Fallis family—mother, father, and four children, aged six, eight, ten, and twelve.

Elder King had another coughing fit as they were walking up to the house, but he seemed to calm down after they were inside. Once, when Elder King did cough again for a few moments, though, Adam, the twelve-year-old, said, "Oh, great, now we all have to get sick because the missionaries want a free meal."

Sister Fallis shushed him immediately, but the boy still glared at the two young men throughout the rest of the dinner. Even Kitty, the ten-year-old, said, "I thought people serving God were supposed to be nice. It's not nice to make other people sick." Sister Fallis shushed her as well, but Elder King looked at Elder Whyte in embarrassment and declined dessert, so they could leave a few minutes sooner.

As they walked back to the bus stop in silence, Elder Whyte couldn't help but reflect on the characters of the kids in the family. The six-year-old had been sweet. The eight-year-old had been neutral. The ten-year-old had been a little rude. And the twelve-year-old had been awful. It had been consistent throughout the whole meal, not just in regard to the coughing. Was there a natural progression away from innocence as a person matured? What hope did Whyte have then by the time he was 25? Or 30?

Elder King suggested some Dual Study when they arrived back at the apartment, but he was soon coughing too much to participate. Elder Whyte suggested a quick trip to the drugstore to get some cough medicine, but Elder King didn't feel up to it, and of course Elder Whyte wasn't allowed to go by himself.

"I think I'll head on to bed early," said Elder King around 8:30. He undressed down to his garments and climbed under the covers. Whyte stayed in the kitchen reading the scriptures for another hour, but he could hear King's increasing bouts of coughing coming from the bedroom.

It never occurred to Elder Whyte to worry about how the coughing might make it difficult for him to get to sleep later himself. He was just worried about helping his companion somehow. Elder King was a decent companion as far as companions went. Elder Whyte liked him.

When he crawled into bed later, he listened to Elder King's continued coughing. At one point, Elder King even moaned to himself, "Oh, I wish I was dead."

Elder Whyte didn't even think about what he did next. He just got up and climbed into the bed beside Elder King.

"What are you doing?"

Whyte put his arm around King. "I'm just going to hold you for a little while, until you fall asleep."

"What?" Elder King went into another coughing fit. When he finally recovered, he spluttered. "Get out of my bed. I'm fine. Sheesh."

Elder Whyte didn't want to get out of the bed, but he figured he had no choice. His own father had held him in his arms back when Elder Whyte had had the mumps as a child. It obviously wasn't just a gay thing to do. Men could be nurturing to each other, couldn't they?

Or was that only family? Was what he had done perverted? Maybe he'd already gone too far beyond the norm to be a decent judge of these things.

Elder Whyte stayed up listening to Elder King's continuous coughing, until they both finally fell asleep exhausted.

The next day was P-Day, so Elder Whyte let his companion sleep in. He went to the kitchen and found that the only thing left in the apartment for breakfast was peanut butter and jelly. He still hoped to do something nice for his birthday later, though. He studied for a while after eating and then wrote letters to some friends, still letting King sleep longer, and finally he had another peanut butter and jelly sandwich for lunch. It was probably all he deserved on his birthday, but he hoped God had something special in store for him at some point in the day. Heavenly Father almost always remembered him on his birthday in some way. It was kind of fun to anticipate it, to keep that youthful sense of excitement. Smiling, he realized with a start that he was now no longer officially a teenager.

By the time Whyte had finished lunch, Elder King awoke groggily and stumbled into the shower. "We have to meet Stan for soccer."

"You're too sick, Elder."

"We can't just leave him hanging. That would be rude."

"We'll walk over and talk to him, but you don't need to be playing ball when you're sick."

King leaned against the wall. "Okay."

Stan arrived at the park just after 1:00, and the missionaries explained why they weren't going to play and apologized. "That's all right. We can do it another time."

"Maybe next week."

"Sure," said Stan, "but listen. The least I can do is give you a blow job in the bushes over there. Someone playing with my snake always makes *me* feel better."

Elder King and Elder Whyte just stared at the man. "You guys *are* gay, aren't you? I've usually got pretty good gaydar."

"No, we're not gay. Come on, Elder Whyte, let's get out of here."

The missionaries turned and left the park, and neither of them spoke as they headed back to the apartment. Elder Whyte felt both a thrill to have met another gay man, and appalled at the same time. How could Stan have said such a thing? Been so crude and disgusting? Stan could only have been a few years older than he was. Was Elder Whyte destined to wallow in a moral gutter by the time he was just twenty-three as well? Maybe each birthday was something to dread, not to celebrate, if it brought him that much closer to absolute wickedness.

As they passed the elementary school near their apartment, the elders were distracted by a small demonstration. But to Elder Whyte's horror, he saw that the signs the circling adults were carrying said things like, "No gay role models," "No to recruitment," "Don't spread the sickness of homosexuality," and "The Bible says no to gays." Apparently, there was a gay teacher at the school, corrupting children who were already becoming sinners at too fast a pace as it was.

Elder Whyte looked at Elder King, who was as pale as a ghost, obviously still feeling very poorly.

But they had hardly gone half a block beyond the school when Elder King suddenly started crying.

"Elder King! Are you okay? What's wrong?"

Elder King sobbed for another few minutes, only stopping when he started another coughing fit. After last night's episode, Elder Whyte didn't know what to do, but he couldn't resist laying his arm across his companion's shoulders.

"What is it?" he asked again, squeezing Elder King's arm.

"It's true!" King sobbed. "What Stan said. I *am* gay." He started to pull away from Elder Whyte but instead turned and put his face against Elder Whyte's shoulder. "Oh, Elder, what am I going to do? I'm going to go to hell."

"No, no," whispered Elder Whyte soothingly. "You're strong. You'll be celibate. You'll be okay."

Elder King sobbed again. "Even if I'm celibate, I won't get into the Celestial Kingdom. Anything short of that is still hell. And I can tell," he said, pulling away and looking Elder Whyte straight in the face, "I can tell I won't stay celibate for long."

Elder Whyte didn't know what to say. He wasn't sure he was brave enough to admit his own gayness, and yet he felt so close to Elder King right now that he had to say something.

"Let's get back to the apartment. You need to rest. We'll talk again after you've taken a nap."

"You—you don't hate me, do you?"

"Of course not, Elder. Everything's going to be all right. We'll think of something."

A few minutes later, Elder Whyte put a cup of milk in the microwave for his companion and then ordered him to bed. Elder King complied listlessly, still sniffling every so often. But soon he was asleep, and Elder Whyte took out his scriptures again.

"Please, God, let me read something that will help me. That will help us both."

He flipped through the scriptures at random a few times and read at length but came upon nothing particularly meaningful. He took a break around 6:00 to have another peanut butter and jelly sandwich, and then he returned to the Book of Mormon. On his twelfth attempt at revelation, he came upon a chapter near the end of Ether. The words struck him like a rod.

"And if men come unto me I will show unto them their weakness. I give unto men weakness that they may be humble; and my grace is sufficient for all men that humble themselves before me; for if they humble themselves before me, and have faith in me, then will I make weak things become strong unto them."

Suddenly, Elder Whyte's mind was filled with images and ideas, scenes of the elementary school kids crossing the street, of little Peter clinging to his leg, of the Catholic woman worrying about Limbo, of Stan propositioning his companion.

Elder Whyte and Elder King were damned to hell almost without a doubt. Neither he nor his companion had enough faith to think they could live respectable lives. Elder Whyte knew they'd both given up two years of their youth to serve the Church, to try against all odds to bring some other souls to God, even if they could never be with Him themselves.

But here in this area, they'd be lucky to baptize ten people in their whole mission. And there was no guarantee that just because someone was baptized they'd live a righteous life. Whyte and King were proof enough of that.

But what if? What *if* there was a way to bring more souls to God? A *surefire* way to bring more souls to Him? Their weakness of being damned could actually become a strength.

Elder Whyte was thinking of an idea. It might mean he and Elder King would go to hell for sure, but that was pretty likely in any event. So why not sacrifice their two already damaged souls entirely to find a definite way to help dozens and dozens of others?

The elementary school was the answer. There must be several first and second grade classrooms filled with children under eight. Every one of those children who died before the age of accountability would go to the Celestial

Kingdom. If their parents truly understood this, they wouldn't likely be overly sad to see their kids go.

No one would even bother to stop two clean cut missionaries from entering the school.

What a great birthday present God had given him, an idea to do something wonderful. It was a grown up present, and Elder Whyte felt touched by it.

He wondered briefly if sacrificing themselves would somehow save them, too, but then he shook his head. This wasn't to help themselves. This was to save the kids. Maybe Herod had been right, after all, in his massacre of innocents. Or was it the massacre of innocence?

Elder Whyte heard his companion stirring in the next room and went to sit on his bed. "How're you feeling, fella?"

Elder King looked up at him and started crying again softly.

"It's okay," said Elder Whyte soothingly. "It's okay."

"How can it possibly be okay?" moaned his companion. He covered his face in his hands.

"Elder," said Whyte, and from the odd tone in his voice, King looked up expectantly. Whyte smiled and looked down at the man, feeling a joy he'd never felt before, clearly a witness that he was without a doubt following the Holy Spirit for a change. "Elder," he said again, running his fingers through Elder King's hair, "I have a plan."

The Hotel Room

When I finished, there was dead silence in the room. I studied Sefton to see how he would react, and he was staring straight ahead, at nothing. I wondered again if I'd gone too far. Treating tumors almost always left some kind of collateral damage, and this was no different. In any event, it was close to dawn now, and even if Sefton wasn't too much of a wreck to go to work, I certainly was. I hoped I could talk my professor into letting me take a make-up exam. Some professors refused outright. I'd hate to have screwed up my GPA just for the sake of one single vote on one single bill, in a political system that was going to keep screwing me over probably for the rest of my life, if not over gay rights, then over universal healthcare or over worker's rights or over the environment or over *something* else important.

"You okay, Sefton?" I reached over and took his hand.

His hand remained lifeless in mine. "Am I like that?" he asked. "Am I that sick?"

I pulled him close. "Yes," I whispered. "Yes, you are. But you don't have to be. Homophobia is one of the diseases we *have* found a complete cure for."

He turned and regarded me with a mixture of hope and desperation in his eyes. "Heal me?" he asked.

"I can do that, Sefton," I said softly. "I can show you documentaries and movies. I can loan you books. I can even eventually introduce you to a few select friends. It *does* get better. I promise."

He nodded. "I want it to get better. I do. I'll do whatever you ask."

I laughed. "Well, the first thing I ask is for you to start thinking for yourself. Don't rely on me. Don't rely on your religion. Don't rely on your political party. Don't rely on anyone else. Think for yourself." I tousled his hair. "But I can give you the materials you'll need to make sound decisions. That much I can do."

"I think I love you, Houston."

I tried not to laugh at his sincerity. "There's plenty of time for that," I said.

"I feel like we ought to have sex one last time before you go. But I don't want to have sex. I want you to tell me all about your schoolwork. And about your best friends. And about your parents. And everything about you."

I got up from the bed and walked over to the desk. I wrote down my full name, my address, and my phone number, my real one on my regular cell phone. "Next Friday at 7:00," I said. "I'm a stickler for promptness, so please be on time."

"I will."

"And what would you like me to prepare for dinner?"

"My favorite meal is paella." He said it almost as if he were embarrassed. "My wife hates it," he added.

I dreaded all the drama that was ahead for both Sefton and for me, but I knew—I hoped, anyway—we'd eventually end up on the good side of that turbulent mess. I also knew that Sefton was no longer just some John, that it mattered to me what happened to him. "Paella it is," I said. I pulled on my underwear and leaned over to give Sefton a kiss.

"I'm scared," said Sefton, "but I'm excited, too."

"That sounds like an honest approach to life." I slipped my T-shirt over my head and then sat down to pull on my socks. Sefton continued to lie on the bed naked. "You know, in my research," I said, adjusting the toe on my left sock, "I work with HeLa cells."

"What's that?"

"Back in the 1950's, a woman named Henrietta Lacks had cancer, and the doctors took some of her cells. Those cells are still alive today, the only truly immortal cell line we have. Most other cell cultures die off during any given research, but these cell lines stay alive forever. Something about the cancer and the viruses working together in the woman's cells. Those cells are *immortal*."

"Hmm," said Sefton.

"The really incredible thing is that a horrible disease like cancer has led to these cells being able to provide marvelous breakthroughs in all sorts of research all over the world to cure and treat all kinds of diseases. Good things can come out of bad things. Good things can come out of the suffering you've experienced."

"I hope so," said Sefton softly. "I hope so." He stared off into the distance while I put my pants on. "At the very least, I'll abstain from voting today." He chuckled. "Sometimes, abstinence is a good thing."

"Sometimes," I agreed.

"And maybe next time something like this comes up, I'll actually have the nerve to vote the way my heart tells me. Be the leader I keep imagining myself to be."

"Maybe so." Now *I* was trying not to think too much. I was afraid to hope for him. But I just couldn't help it. I tied my shoes and picked up my bag of accessories. Then I leaned over to kiss Sefton one last time.

"See you Friday," he said, smiling. "And have some more stories ready."

I nodded and headed out the door for the elevator, feeling energized. I walked briskly through the lobby and out onto the sidewalk, smiling at the early morning sun. I'd have a quick bite to eat and then head to campus to take my exam. Something told me I just might ace it today, after all.

www.ingramcontent.com/pod-product-compliance
Lightning Source LLC
Chambersburg PA
CBHW021146310726

48971CB00002B/513